The Reunion

Matt Bircher

ISBN-13: 978-0-578-36998-3

Front Cover designed by Stephanie W. Dicken
Back Cover photo by Holly Desrosier
Formatting by Polgarus Studio

To all of my cousins …
who make every moment in their presence memorable.

Acknowledgments

Writing my fourth and most personal novel was very fulfilling. I thank God for the experiences and people that made this story unfold into what it has become. It is a blessing to have this creative outlet to share with others. To my parents, Scott and Emma Bircher, I am so thankful for your never ending love and support which has always remained constant. My sister Maggie, thank you for using your creative gifts to inspire me. To my grandparents, Joe and Linda Thomas, I am always appreciative of your support and my time spent with you. To the book's first reader, Linda Thomas, "MeMe", thank you for taking the time to be a part of this process. My grandparents, Jack and Julia Bircher, your spirit is always uplifting and encouraging. I am beyond grateful for that. To Sharon Bland, who always reveals the book's potential with your revisions and expertise, thank you for your availability and commitment. To every other family member and friend in my life, you are all the greatest gift to me and an amazing source for support. If you're reading this, know that you are a valuable piece of a puzzle that has grown further than I could have ever imagined. To everyone who has made it complete, I truly do thank you.

Introduction

A trail of dust faded into the air along the dirt road that seemed to have no end. Leading the way was Roy Webster's white pick-up truck. It was traveling at a much faster speed than it ever had on this particular road. Seated in the passenger seat, Roy Webster still felt that it was not fast enough.

"Pick up the pace!" he said to the driver as he turned around and looked out the truck's back window.

"Sir, nobody's chasing us. Relax." the driver said.

"We don't know for sure with all of that dust behind us ... what did I tell you about calling me 'Sir'?" Roy asked.

"Sorry ... *Dad*."

Roy Webster frantically turned back around, this time without glancing out the window. Instead, he looked at the large storage trunk that had been placed in the back seat to make sure it was still there. At the same time, the driver attempted to capture Mr. Webster's short-spanned attention.

"Sir ... I mean ... Dad. What's the purpose of this?" the driver asked.

Seeing that the trunk was safely buckled in, per his request, Roy briefly took his eyes off of it to respond.

"I'll tell you when we get to the lake ... just keep going."

There were good reasons the driver struggled to call Roy Webster "Dad." The biggest being that it had been less than a year since they first met. Unwilling and lacking the patience to interfere with Mr. Webster's mind that had become as foggy as the view behind them, the driver simply went along with his commands. Eddie Brewer's task of spending time with Roy Webster on this particular day had turned into something very much unexpected. Eddie never seemed to be on the same page as Roy Webster, nor was anyone else at this point in the elderly gentleman's life. Yet he still found himself behind the wheel in a scenario that had been concocted in thoughts filled with paranoia. If Eddie had known that this was what "watching" Mr. Webster for the day meant, he would have most definitely reconsidered.

The two would have had no reason to know each other had it not been for one person who was responsible for putting Eddie in this strange position. Her name was Carolyn Webster-Brewer, the daughter of Roy Webster and the newly wedded wife of Eddie Brewer. Still, that connection had nothing to do with Mr. Webster's wish for his son-in-law to call him "Dad." It was the fact that he had two sons of his own, both middle-aged men such as Eddie. This gave Mr. Webster every reason to believe that he was one of the two. Which one? Roy Webster did not care in that particular moment … he did not have a clue. All that mattered, as his eyes remained fixed on the trunk, was getting to the lake at a rapid pace.

When they finally approached the line of trees that had once appeared so distant, the truck came to a halt before continuing on through the small opening.

"What's the matter?" Roy asked after facing forward.

Looking at the crossroads they had come upon in the wooded path, Eddie replied, "There's three choices … well, four if you count just putting this thing in reverse and taking you and your big treasure box thing back home."

Hearing no immediate response from Mr. Webster, Eddie decided to do just that. While he reached his hand down to the gear shift, Roy immediately reached his left arm out and slapped his hand away.

After experiencing the brief touch of Mr. Webster's cold, clammy hand, Eddie looked at him and asked, "Well?"

Eddie, having never been to the Webster lake compound in his short time with the family, lacked any idea of what was beyond the dirt road. He felt sure that Mr. Webster would have no more sense of direction in the wooded area than he did. What he underestimated was the natural instincts that over fifty years' of Mr. Webster's visits to one place had produced.

"Right, left, right." Mr. Webster mumbled under his breath before repeating himself in the same tone, "Right, left, right."

Almost certain that the words he could barely hear had no meaning, Eddie asked, "What? Sir, speak up a little."

Mr. Webster turned around and saw the dust beginning to settle behind them. Becoming impatient with the extended lack of movement, Mr. Webster sternly replied loud and clear, "Turn right, Boy."

Though he had never heard that kind of assurance from his father-in-law before, Eddie still could not manage to find an ounce of confidence in Mr. Webster's direction.

"Go!" Roy said while facing Eddie closer than ever.

It was seeing the growing look of fury in Mr. Webster's eyes that pushed Eddie to give in and turn right. He could already begin to imagine their pictures on lost persons' posters as he made the turn. He followed the directions, and much to his surprise, the wooded path opened up to a spacious cleared area after the final right turn. In addition to the body of water that appeared ahead of them, a wooden cottage could be seen front and center. It was built on a slope to overlook the lake below. Mr. Webster began pointing toward it.

"Drive over to the house." he said to Eddie.

Eddie did just that; and when the truck pulled into the gravel driveway, Mr. Webster opened the glovebox. He dug around in it for a few seconds and seemed to be having no luck finding what he was looking for.

"Having trouble, Sir?" asked Eddie

"The key. I can't find the key to get in."

"Is it the same key you put in your shirt pocket earlier?"

Mr. Webster looked at Eddie as he reached in his shirt pocket and pulled out the key to the cottage. Gripping it tightly in his hand, Mr. Webster did not skip a beat as he quickly got out of the truck. Eddie, at a less rushed pace, did the same thing as he took in the view of the surrounding lake that he was seeing for the first time.

"Quite a place you have back here." he yelled over to Mr. Webster. By this time, he was already halfway up the cottage porch steps.

Without acknowledging Eddie's words, Mr. Webster, with one hand on the rail, turned to face him as he said, "How about bringing that trunk inside for me?"

Eddie let out a sigh as he remembered the trouble he had gone through getting it in the truck's back seat earlier. Seeing the added challenge of hauling it up the set of stairs that led to the tall front deck did not intrigue him in any way. However, continuing with the day's trend, Eddie did as Mr. Webster asked as if there were no other options.

After squeezing the trunk through the front doorway to the cottage, he saw that Mr. Webster's sense of urgency lessened after he closed the cottage door. The blank look on his face hinted that he had possibly forgotten his reason for being there, something Eddie was not so sure of himself. They stood in silence for a moment in the foyer which was lit only by the natural light from outside. Eddie gently sat the trunk down.

"Is this it?" he asked.

Mr. Webster looked out of a nearby window and responded, "I think we have some time."

"Oh, do we? Is that so?" Eddie sarcastically asked in response to Mr. Webster's sudden change in his mode.

"Follow me." Mr. Webster said as he began to walk down a hallway.

Eddie bent down and picked up the trunk for what he hoped would be the last time. He eased down the dark hallway behind Mr. Webster who peaked his head in every room. It was not until they reached the last door in the hall that he opened it all the way and walked inside. Eddie remained in the hall and watched as the elderly man reached for the room's closet door handle and opened it.

"Right here." Mr. Webster said aloud as he signaled Eddie over while saying, "Put it right in here."

Eddie entered the bedroom that housed three bunk beds and hoped this strange saga was coming to an end, but he was not yet off the hook. Seeing that the closet was completely full, he paused and questioned, "I'm supposed to put this thing in here?"

"There's always room for more."

"Yeah, but-"

"Make room. Pile it up. It'll be safe here."

Eddie reluctantly sat the trunk down once again. He removed several boxes and other miscellaneous items piled on the floor. Once a space big enough for the trunk was cleared, Eddie, refusing to pick it up again, pushed it up against a wall in the back corner of the closet. While Mr. Webster took a look outside through the room's small window, Eddie stacked the items that he had removed on and around the trunk.

"Okay, sir." Eddie said as he exhaled after a deep breath.

"The perfect spot for it." Mr. Webster said about the trunk that was buried in the closet. "Now let's go."

Back in the truck, Eddie drove up the dirt road in no hurry. His mind was replaying everything that had just happened. He found that his thoughts were much clearer without having to process the chaotic orders that had he been given constantly on the drive to the cottage.

Wanting to make sense of it all, he was compelled to blurt out the question, "What was that all about?"

"What is 'that'?" asked Mr. Webster.

Eddie replied, "Well, 'that' being whatever just happened back there."

"Uh-well ... uh-mmm ..."

"The trunk!" Eddie straightforwardly clarified as his frustration level continued to rise. "Yeah?" asked Mr. Webster.

"That's what I'm talking about."

"You don't know what that is?" the elder man quibbled.

"No. No, Sir I do not."

"Well, I thought you did, Son." said Mr. Webster. "You said it earlier ... treasure."

"Treasure? Yeah, okay." Eddie replied, remembering the sarcastic remark that he had made about the trunk earlier.

"I'm serious." Mr. Webster said, "What is in that box will take care of this family long after Helen and I are gone."

The mention of Helen, Mr. Webster's wife of over fifty years, allowed Eddie to remember the high financial standing that the couple had built for themselves. The power that came along with that was immense, as was the opportunity that Eddie quickly pictured for himself.

"Is that so?" he asked Mr. Webster as his selfish desires began to brew.

"Of course, my Boy ... of course."

It was all making sense to Eddie now that he connected that explanation to the reason for Mr. Webster's intense care of the trunk. If, in fact, the items inside of it were as valuable as Mr. Webster described them, Eddie knew the perfect reward had fallen right into his lap. After he had spent the day putting up with the old man's orders, Eddie could think of nobody more deserving of inside knowledge on the trunk's new location and possession of everything in it.

Mr. Webster continued, "Now, make sure your brother and sister are in on this too. It concerns all three of you."

Brother and sister? Eddie thought to himself as he temporarily forgot the role in which he was playing front and center.

"Oh-yeah ... Dad. I'll do that." he replied as his head cleared.

"And don't think I didn't hear all of those "Sirs" back there in the house." said Mr. Webster.

"My manners got the best of me, I guess." Eddie replied.

"I see."

Eddie, meaning many things, replied, "I don't think it will happen again." ... "No more manners." he continued quietly under his breath.

When they reached the end of the dirt road and turned onto the main highway, Eddie was already looking forward to his next visit ... a visit that would serve as ... *the reunion.*

Chapter 1

Months later ...

Cars filled the funeral home parking lot late on a Saturday afternoon. The line of people waiting to get inside stretched outside of the front doors. With a crowd so large, many of them would be forced to gather around a television in a separate room from the chapel to watch the service. Most everyone there knew Roy Webster, some better than others. His personality and reputation was such that one meeting with him caused a connection strong enough to cause people to want to celebrate his long and well-lived life.

Inside the chapel, Colin Webster, Roy's only grandson, glanced back from his front row seat to see every row behind him filled. A pianist softly played music as people gathered. By the time the music stopped, everyone had taken their seats. Colin now looked straight ahead as the room grew quiet. It was his cue to take the stage. Feeling the tight squeeze of his mother's hand, he stood from his seat and swiftly made his way up to the podium. Colin had been told that the eulogy was not his to give ... only a few words to begin the service were needed. As a news reporter from the local paper, jotting down a "few words" was no problem for him. The difference came from the method of research required to put the words on paper. There was only one source that could be accessed for this occasion ... the memories that filled his heart.

Before speaking, Colin looked down to the wooden podium as he removed and unfolded the paper from his suit pocket and put it in place. He placed both hands on the podium and looked up to see every eye in the crowded room on him. Colin's eyes immediately shifted his focus to the lone empty seat next to his mother where he had been seated. His mother, Carolyn, was noticeably shaken, more so than her two brothers, their families, and even her own mother who had just lost her husband. They felt as if they had lost Roy long ago since he had not been the same man that everyone had known all those years before. For Carolyn it was different. She had been the one who had cared for him day in and day out, often finding little moments throughout that time which allowed her to still see a glimpse of Roy's true beloved personality that had faded. She was the one person who could pull it out of him.

It pained Colin to see his mother in that state. He knew the reasons behind her emotions went beyond the loss of her father. Carolyn's husband, Eddie, had left their family after less than a year of marriage, a decision that would have played out much differently if it had been her choice. That was why Colin wished to be the one person by her side. It was a place he had held throughout his entire life. The seat beside her would remain open until the words on the page in front of him were spoken.

"Friends." Colin said as he spoke into the microphone while looking at the crowd. "Family." he continued as he looked back to the first two rows where his two uncles, aunts, and six cousins were seated.

He took a good look at them, the Webster family, and saw a group of people who were on the verge of becoming estranged. Though sitting closely together, they were very far apart in their own immediate family bubbles. The family patriarch and matriarch, Roy and Helen Webster, had always been the backbone that held them together. As they grew older, the Webster family's once strong foundation had drastically weakened. The change occurred slowly over time; and nobody, not even most members of the family, had seen this happening. However, from Colin's observant perspective it was very clear.

"For Roy Webster, my grandfather … there is no more pain. He is no longer a prisoner of his own mind. He has been set free. My grandfather's story began and ended with his family, whom he loved dearly. To know him, you had to know all of us … the Websters."

When he heard himself say that final sentence, Colin knew that there was very little truth to it. Even he, who spent countless hours with his grandfather, did not truly know his family. There was once a time when he thought he did — good times that seemed so authentic. It was to that place in time that Colin's mind rested. In the midst of facing how life had actually turned out, he focused now on how it had once been.

Chapter 2

Christmas Eve many years before ...

Past the mailbox with "Webster" emblazoned on the side of it and the driveway filled with parked cars was the Webster family Christmas gathering. Though the lights were wrapped around every piece of landscape to illuminate the home's exterior, the sight inside was even brighter. With everyone's stomachs filled after dinner and dessert, they all gathered in the living room. Roy and Helen sat in their respective recliners while the others found their usual seats. Some had to pull chairs from the kitchen table into the sitting area.

After the family had formed a big circle and everyone had started chatting, Helen interrupted to ask, "Does everyone remember their parts?"

Tony Webster, her oldest son, replied, "I remember, Mom. We do this every year."

"Just making sure." Helen replied. Turning toward her husband, she asked, "Roy, do you remember our part?"

"Oh, uh-yeah of course. I'll just follow your lead." he replied.

"Can't we just open the presents already?" asked one of the younger cousins who was looking longingly at the wide array of gifts under and scattered around the large Christmas tree.

Charlie Webster, the cousin's father, signaled for his youngest daughter to come join everyone and said, "We have to earn those presents with our singing voices ... okay?"

"That's right." Helen said, "Okay! Ready?" she asked excitingly.

"Are *you* ready?" Colin Webster asked his cousin, Mary, who sat next to him.

"You know it. I hope you are … it's our show to steal." Mary replied.

Without any further prompting, all fifteen voices combined as they began. *Onnnnn … the first day of Christmas my true love gave to me …*

Colin and Mary did not have to wait too long for their line of "*two turtle doves*" to begin. As they gave different renditions of those words every time, the part suited the duo very well. Saying the word "*two*" itself was perfect for Colin and Mary who did almost everything imaginable together. Truly joined at the hip, the two cousins not only happened to be the same age and had been in every class together since kindergarten, they were also best friends. Colin and Mary thought very much alike and seemed to always be on the same frequency. It was a common occurrence for them to say "*same brain!*" when they finished each other's sentences. To those around them, both in the school and family settings, their special connection was very well recognized. Nonstop laughs and meaningless jokes that only the two of them understood made their close relationship obvious.

"*… a partridge in a pear tree!*" All the voices sung together as one.

Everyone clapped and cheered as the "*Twelve Days of Christmas*" came to an end. It had been filled with humorous acts and mishaps which they laughingly recounted. Alas, it was time to open the gifts. Thus, the lengthy process of getting them all passed out to the rightful recipients began. When every gift was in the correct possession and after the count of three, all were torn open at the same time. It was not long before the living room floor was filled with torn wrapping paper, bows and box lids. The atmosphere, and the family within it, remained full of love and cheer … without any of them recognizing how fragile those feelings could be.

Christmas Eve … two years after Roy's funeral.

Past the mailbox with "Webster" emblazoned on the side of it and the driveway filled with parked cars was a sign mounted beside the front door that read, "Webster Inn." Those same words in an identical, but much larger font, were on a sign by the road. Lights were again wrapped around every piece of landscape that illuminated the exterior of the Webster homestead. They seemed to be even brighter than they had been when the home's owners, Roy and Helen, were still living there. Inside, the large Christmas tree still stood tall … front and center … fully decorated. However, it lacked any sign of wrapped presents under or around it. Every piece of furniture was in the same place as it had always been. The only notable difference was the people who happened to be seated there.

For the two people upstairs, such a thing took some getting used to. It was Colin and his mother, Carolyn, who helplessly listened to the loud noise coming from the guests on the floor below. Hosting strangers in the family home was only one of the many adjustments they had been forced to make. The biggest was their living quarters being confined to the space above the garage. It included a small kitchenette and one bathroom which the two of them shared. Because of the nonstop workload that came along with operating a bed and breakfast facility, they were too busy to spend very much time in the room. Whether it was cooking breakfast for the guests, changing bed sheets, cleaning, or maintaining the property that had been left behind, there was always something for the mother and son to do.

Gathered around a small Christmas tree that was tucked away in one of the room's corners, Colin and Carolyn had no choice but to spend Christmas Eve night in their cramped space. They sat on the floor while exchanging the few gifts they got for each other. Colin had just reached under the tree for the final gift when they were interrupted by a loud noise as if something or someone had fallen. It was followed by an eruption of laughter coming from the crowd of people downstairs.

"Okay!" Colin said as he set the present aside and began to stand up, "I'm going down there. This is too much."

"Now, you know that's not going to help anything. Last time it just made things worse." Carolyn reminded her son.

She continued, "Let's just try to make the best of it. That's all we can do … it's what we *have* to do."

After a brief moment of reflection, Colin sat back down. He wondered if it was really worth putting himself through this. After obtaining a college degree, he had chosen to move back home to help his mother care for her aging parents. Now with them both gone, Colin recognized that he had not realized the heavy weight of the responsibilities that were handed over to the next generation. He felt there was no way he could leave his mother to handle them alone.

Carolyn said to her son, "You can proceed with that gifting." as she eyed the wrapped box by the tree.

"Oh, yeah." Colin said as he reached for it again. While handing it over, he told her, "It's nothing pricey like you deserve but ...."

"If it's from you I'm sure it's special." Carolyn replied as she carefully removed the bow and began pulling off the wrapping paper.

She opened the box to see a framed photo of the two of them pictured alongside her parents. The picture had been taken years before during the Webster family's former Christmas Eve traditional gathering. Tears filled her eyes as she examined it closely.

"Well ... would you look at that!" she said. "It's priceless." She continued to stare intently at the photo.

"If only we had known just how good those days were while we were living them." said Colin in a somber voice.

The photo offered a sobering glimpse of their present reality which was in stark contrast to years past when they were among family in the living room downstairs. Now most evenings turned into hearing guests getting acquainted with each other and most often enjoying themselves a little too much downstairs.

The question "*WHY?*" was one that surfaced in their minds quite often as they pondered their current situation. To answer that question would require them going back to the day when everything changed for the Webster family.

One of the final Webster family gatherings had been less than a year after Roy had passed away. When everyone met at the homestead that year, they each knew Helen would soon be joining Roy. With steadily declining health since her husband's funeral, there was very little that the hospice care workers could do to help her. In what were deemed her final hours, the family was well aware of the inevitable. That awareness allowed for one of her three children to begin planning ahead by plotting out the second generation's future paths that would include very little interaction with each other.

It was another day in a week filled with extended family and friends floating in and out of the house to fill the kitchen with meals and the home with comfort and support. In the later hours of the night after all the visitors had left, everyone in the Webster family sat around Helen's bedside knowing very well that it was only a matter of time before her final breath would be taken.

They all watched as Carolyn sat closest to her mother's ear and quietly recounted the many happy memories from her lifetime. Helen looked as peaceful as she had been in a long time. The serenity of the moment was suddenly broken when the doorbell sounded. Carolyn's oldest brother, Tony, who stood near the bedroom door, looked down at his watch to see that it was quite late for another visitor to arrive.

"I'll get it." he said while making his way out of the crowded room, wondering who could be at the door. His younger brother, Charlie, curiously trailed behind him at a distance. Just before Tony got to the front entrance, the doorbell sounded once again.

"Coming!" said Tony while picking up the pace and reaching to unlock the door.

As he opened the door, Tony began to speak, "Look, now is not the best time ..." Then he recognized the gentlemen standing before him as one the family's lawyers.

"Oh ... it's you. I didn't think you were coming now."

"I'm sorry it's so late, I had a few other stops along the way that took longer than expected. I tried to call earlier." the visitor said.

"Oh, yeah. No ... it's been a hectic day, and none of us has been near a phone ... just people, and a lot of them."

"I understand. I can come back another time if that works out better for the family." said the man.

After Tony took a quick look back to see his brother watching, he turned back to the gentlemen standing on the front porch and assured him, "No, it's fine. Come on in."

"Great, I'll be right in. I just need to grab a few things." he said as he made his way back to his car which was parked along the circle driveway.

As Tony turned toward his brother, Charlie asked him, "What's his name again?"

"I don't recall. It's Mom and Dad's estate lawyer ... that's the only title that matters."

"Do you think now is really the best time to begin this?" asked Charlie.

Tony replied, "The sooner this process begins, the better ... for all of us."

"I don't know if Carolyn is going to feel too good about doing this right now. I don't even know if I do!" Charlie responded.

"Hmmm. Well, suit yourself." said Tony.

Knowing all too well of his brother's manipulative capabilities, Charlie replied, "I'll be right back." as he went to let Carolyn in on what was happening.

Leaving her mother's bedside seconds later, she stormed into the living room with Charlie just as the lawyer made his way inside the open door holding a paper box in his hands.

"Really? Are you serious?" Carolyn asked Tony, who was sitting comfortably on one of the couches.

"I'm assuming you two are the other siblings?" stated the lawyer.

"Yes." Carolyn said sternly before asking, "And what is your name?"

"I'm Greg Norman, your parents' estate attorney. Tony called my office to arrange a few meetings to discuss the will ... I'm sorry for your loss. I heard a lot about Ms. Helen from your father over the years. They were good people."

"We haven't lost her!!" said Carolyn.

"No?" asked Greg.

"She's in the other room ... would you like to see her?" Carolyn sneered in response.

"What my sister means is that we haven't lost her *yet* ... and we're just wanting to take these first steps."

"I cannot believe you." Carolyn said to Tony. "I have every right to ... but this is low even for your standards."

"Relax, don't be stuck in denial." he said to her.

At that point everyone else but Colin had left Helen's bedroom as the sound of Carolyn's voice in the other room became increasingly louder and more irritable. Her son had no interest in a confrontation and took his mother's seat closest to Helen's bed. The others got to the living room just in time to stop Carolyn from totally erupting.

"What's going on?" Charlie's wife asked, speaking for the other family members who came from Helen's bedside and stood behind her.

Before Carolyn could answer, Greg pleaded, "Everybody just take a moment to calm down." Hoping to gain control of the room, he continued, "I do not want this to be any more difficult than it has to be."

With everyone's full attention on him, the lawyer speaking authoritatively said, "I need everyone to take a seat with their respective families if they're here so there is no confusion."

Those who had just entered the living room took seats while Carolyn remained standing.

Before Mr. Norman continued he asked her, "Could you please take a seat, ma'am?"

"My mother cannot be left by herself ... I don't even know why I'm out here." she said as she began to walk back toward the bedroom.

"I think Colin is in there." said one of her nieces.

"It's okay." Greg said, "This will not take long; it's just an introduction to the process. Then I'll be on my way."

Back in Helen's bedroom, Colin watched his grandmother closely while she slowly breathed in and out. His mind took in mental images of every detail of her face that he hoped to never forget. Colin noticed that her peaceful demeanor from minutes earlier had turned into a look of distress and pain as if she sensed what was going on in the other room. Badly wanting to sooth whatever thoughts were floating around in his grandmother's head, Colin gently placed one hand on both of hers that were folded on her stomach and softly rubbed his thumb back and forth over Helen's wrinkled skin.

"What's gotten into them." Colin whispered to himself just before noticing one of his grandmother's eyelids peep open.

Shortly afterward, the other eye opened, Helen murmured, "Wha … What now?"

Wide eyed, Colin responded, "No-no … nothing."

"Something. Always something." she said as she shook her head from side to side.

Helen unfolded her hands and pointed toward the nightstand beside her. In a weak and whispered voice, she said to Colin, "Get a pen … pen and paper."

Colin opened and rummaged through the drawer and chose one of the many pens and a pad of paper that were in it.

After testing the pen, he rummaged back in the drawer and tested several pens before finding one that would work. He handed it over toward his grandmother thinking that she was going to write something. However, instead of taking the pen, she closed her eyes once again. Several seconds went by, and Colin was just about to place the pen and pad of paper back in the drawer when Helen spoke unexpectedly.

"The key." she said with her eyes still closed.

Colin paused and did a double take. He asked, "What's that?"

Helen opened both eyes and focused them on the paper in his hands.

"Write." she said, losing the strength to keep her eyes opened, "The key. Search begins where flowers bloom and ends in a song sung. Family together again."

Colin did not write anything and instead looked at his grandmother in a pure state of bewilderment. He knew those words were the most she had pieced together in a long time … but with that came the realization that they could not have had any less of a meaning.

Helen took another look at her grandson and the blank piece of paper he held, and then she began to lose control of her emotions. Seeing his grandmother in tears, Colin quickly stood up to call for help, dropping the pen and paper on the bed.

"Don't." Helen said.

Colin stood still in his tracks. The tone in her voice proved her state of mind had some credibility left.

"*Don't you dare.*" she grumbled.

Colin turned around to see the pen and pad of paper in Helen's feeble hands. He slowly approached the bed again as he watched her attempt to draw something out. Her shaky hand produced a crooked circle near the top of the page. Beginning at the bottom of the circle was a skinny rectangular shape. She left a small space and began to draw another misshapen circle further down on the paper followed by the same skinny rectangular shape. By the time she set the pen aside and signaled Colin closer, there were three of them lined up vertically on the page.

Leaning her head all the way back to face the ceiling, Helen told Colin, "You're different."

Acting as if he did not hear her, Colin said nothing. Instead, he reached for the paper to take a closer look.

Even though he knew a solid answer would not be given, he asked, "What's this?"

"Listen." Helen said as her voice weakened. "You're different."

"Different?"

"You're different because you never changed ... you stayed here. You never left."

Colin began to respond, "Oh-well ... I ..." Then Helen chimed in, "The key ... *keys*. The search ... the search begins where flowers bloom. It ends in a song sung. Keys lined up old to young. Family together again." Colin was smart enough to write down the words that his grandmother repeated that time. She had repeated the same words twice, and that gave him a strong indication that those words may mean something after all.

By the time he finished jotting down Helen's words on the other side of the paper before he forgot them, Colin looked up to see that she was completely out of it. It was as if she had poured out everything within herself to say what needed to be said. He sat down and reassessed their talk. He looked at her drawing with an entirely new perspective. Recalling Helen's heavy emphasis on the word "key," Colin no longer saw three circles with thin rectangular bottoms, but instead keyholes that were vertically aligned.

Ah, of course ... that's it. he thought.

"Is she okay?" a voice that he recognized as his mother's asked from behind him.

Colin turned around and stood up, "Oh, I think so. Just sleeping."

"Has she said anything at all?" his mother asked while she walked closer to Helen's bed.

"Uhm ... not too much." Colin said as he ripped the piece of paper from the pad proving that his response had been misleading.

Placing the paper in his pocket, Colin continued, "Here, I was in your seat." He saw the look of exhaustion on his mother's face.

As she began to sit down, Carolyn said to him, "If there's anyone around here that I can trust to be in my place, it's you."

"Well, of course. I'm your son."

"That and you're not schmoozing up to the lawyer guy out there." replied Carolyn.

"I thought they'd all be gone by now." said Colin, referring to the other family members.

"They pretty much are now." Carolyn said, "I think they made their mental exit as soon as the guy in a suit mentioned money and possessions."

Changing the subject, Carolyn asked, "Anyways, have you heard anything from Mary? Her dad said she was planning to stop by at some point."

"Oh, really?" Colin pulled out his phone and replied, "No I haven't." ignoring the fact that he did not even have his cousin's number.

"Oh, okay."

Colin was quick to ask, "Did he say what time? Or?"

"No. You'll have to ask him." Carolyn replied.

Wanting to know more from his Uncle Tony, Mary's father, Colin left the bedroom. He walked past the living room area but stopped at the sight of his family doing exactly what his mother had said. Seeing them treat the lawyer to one of the available meals in the kitchen put a sour taste in his mouth. He knew that his mother was the only one of them who stayed to care for his grandmother ... the woman they were all soon to be without.

"Colin!" said Tony upon seeing him, "Come try some of this pie."

Without saying a word, Colin slowly backed away to rejoin his mother ... unwilling and simply unable to miss his grandmother's last moments with them ... moments which the others had seemed to forget about so easily.

Chapter 3

Helen's funeral came and went, as did many visitors and tin foil wrapped meals which had been packed in the refrigerator. Just as the family felt as if they could finally catch their breath in the weeks after, the estate lawyer, Greg Norman, rang the doorbell of the home for a second time. When the front door opened and he saw who was at the door, Colin realized that he was the only one who was disappointed. He had really hoped it would be his cousin, Mary, there for the visitation, funeral, and every event that was a part of the family memorial time. Whenever the possibility of her attending was mentioned, Colin could only imagine what it would be like to have her there. This would again be another disappointment, but he couldn't help but wish for her to be there.

With most of the family gathered in the living room anxiously awaiting his appearance, Greg Norman had no trouble getting everyone's attention. Even Colin, seated beside his mother, Carolyn, brushed his feelings aside in anticipation of what was to come. When Greg opened his briefcase to scan through his stack of papers, he looked up to see everyone leaning forward in their seats. All eyes were focused solely on him.

"Okay, everyone. Today we'll focus on property only because, as you know, Roy and Helen sure did own a lot of it." said Greg.

He continued, "There are three homes in total that Mr. and Mrs. Webster owned. One being where we find ourselves today, the main residence. The other two served as vacation spots. One is locally known as the lake house, and the other one is a beach house at Harbor Pointe Beach. Is all of this information correct?"

Everyone, without saying anything, nodded their heads.

"Great." said Greg, "Well, this does not happen often, but there are three homes; and, speaking directly to Mr. and Mrs. Webster's children, there are three of you."

As if they didn't see what was coming, the siblings who were seated with their individual families on separate couches gave blank looks to the lawyer.

Dumbing it down, Greg said to them, "In other words, each will be getting a house."

Each of the siblings' blank looks turned into wide eyes.

Before they could ask anything or wrap their heads around what was just said, Greg explained, "I know that is a big deal, but I assure you there is no pressure. You can do what you please with the home and land you acquire from this will. Sell it, rent it out, live there permanently ... you name it."

Tony, the oldest of the siblings, spoke up, "There's a big difference in each house. Who is getting what?"

"Tony, your name is with the lake house. Because it is of less value than the other two, you will also inherit the tree farm and land that surrounds it."

Looking down at the paper again, without seeing any reaction, Greg continued, "Charlie, yours is the beach house at Harbor Pointe; and Carolyn, well, I guess we're all guests of yours. The Webster homestead is now officially in your name."

With that came a collective gasp from everyone, including Carolyn ... especially Carolyn.

Gaining her composure, she spoke up, "Uh-um ... me? This house?"

Just as Greg began to answer, Tony stood up and broke in, "Exactly ... her? *This* house?" while waving his arms to show the large scope of the interior.

Greg excused the children of the siblings who were present from the living room. As all the others happily left, Colin went upstairs.

"Look." Greg said, notably uncomfortable while placing the papers back into his briefcase, "I thought the same thing ... and trust me ... I double checked with both Mr. and Mrs. Webster about their intentions."

Tony replied, "This is a six-bedroom house. There's only one of her ...

plus her sidekick son. That's two. Charlie and I each have three kids … daughters, meaning three weddings and-"

"Oh, Tony, sit down!" his wife said while tugging his shirt.

Before taking his seat, Tony turned to his brother, Charlie, and asked, "Isn't this something?" It was more than obvious that he felt they both got a raw deal.

Charlie, with his cellphone out, was noticeably more content than his brother. No longer on the edge of his seat, he sat back comfortably. Looking up from his phone, he replied, "What's that? Sorry, I'm trying to get up with my realtor to put the house on the market."

"My point exactly." Tony said, "Selling the beach house!! Just like Carolyn will sell this one and walk away doing pretty good!!"

"No." Charlie replied, "Our current house. You can find us at Harbor Pointe."

Carolyn chimed in and asked Tony, "What makes you think I'm selling?"

"I don't see how you have any other option." replied Tony.

"Well, I'll have to find one. This is home … for all of us … not just me." Carolyn responded.

Greg asked Tony, "So your concern is about value, not space. Is that right?"

"Value has a lot to do with space." Tony answered.

"Right. Do you need me to remind you about all the acreage of land that surrounds the lake house that is now in your name?"

Tony reluctantly took his seat as if he felt there was nothing else that was worth saying.

Greg gathered his papers and brief case; but before making his exit, he told the siblings, "I understand this is a complicated process in a difficult time for the family, but this is what has to be done. It is only the beginning, so I will get in touch with you all about future meetings."

From the upstairs landing, Colin listened to the entire exchange while remaining out of sight. Noticing how the downstairs room grew very quiet, Colin looked through an upstairs window that faced the front driveway below. He watched the lawyer walking toward his parked car, and saw him stop and turn around.

It was Carolyn who had casually arisen from the couch and left the tense atmosphere of the living room. Both of her brothers and their spouses, though in different ways, were equally distracted by the news and had failed to notice her follow the lawyer outside.

"Sir." she said after closing the front door behind her.

"Yes, ma'am?" Greg hesitantly asked.

"Don't worry." Carolyn said, "I'm not going to shoot the messenger."

"Your brother already pretty much took care of that." Greg chuckled, "Did you have a question?"

"Kind of … I don't really know. This all just doesn't make much sense to me." Carolyn said as she turned to glance back at the house, "I mean-"

"I understand that it's a lot." Greg replied, "But honestly, after talking to both of your parents, it makes perfect sense."

"Oh?"

"I didn't want to say this inside to stir any further controversy, but from what I could gather, it's you who has always been the most attentive to your parents. Your consistency obviously built their trust."

Carolyn believed that to be true. She knew how much of her time in recent years had been dedicated to her parents and taking care of the things they could no longer do for themselves.

Greg continued, "Frankly, they trusted that you could keep this house a home."

Over 3 years later

It was yet another day when Carolyn rose early and felt far from home while answering her phone.

"Webster-" Carolyn said before clearing her morning voice and starting over, "Webster Inn. This is Carolyn. How may I help you?"

"Yes." the voice on the other end of the line responded, "My husband and I are planning a trip to the historic town of Castwell. I see your bed and breakfast is only ten minutes from that area. Is that true?"

"Yes, we're just off the highway that will bring you right to it."

"Okay. Do you have any rooms available next month?"

"Oh, yes." Carolyn replied, as she sat up and reached for her schedule book that was nearly empty.

"Good to know. I will get in touch with you soon about specific dates ... hopefully before you fill up."

"Great!" Carolyn said just as she heard the disconnect tone through the speaker.

After placing her phone back on the nightstand, she took another look at the schedule book. Speaking aloud to herself, she said, "Fill up? I wish." She tossed the book aside and rubbed her eyes. She let out a big yawn as she checked her watch and then heard a knock on the door.

"You up?" asked Colin from outside.

"Yep."

"You decent?" he asked before opening, as he did every morning, having learned his lesson the hard way once before.

"As decent as I can be." his mother assured him.

Colin walked in from the door that led to what used to be part of the attic. After fully ventilating it, he had spent much of his spare time creating his bedroom there. It had just enough room for a bed and small desk and could be accessed from wooden steps in the garage below.

He went into the small bathroom that he shared with his mother. As he put toothpaste on his toothbrush, Colin asked his mother, "Was that someone wanting a room?" making reference to the phone call he had overheard.

"I think so, but you know how that is. Some say they'll call back but never do." she answered.

"Recently it seems that most people do that." Colin said.

"You know, business shifts up and down depending on the seasons of year."

"Summer will be here before you know it ... we're usually packed by now. You may want to start moving your things into the empty master suite downstairs. I can't remember the last time someone has stayed in there."

"Oh, no. Things will pick up ... We can only hope." his mother said trying to assure him.

Colin put the toothbrush back on the bathroom counter as he turned to her and shared some insight he had as a local journalist.

"Not if all those new bed and breakfast openings in downtown Castwell have anything to say about it. Especially since they're only walking distance from the places tourists want to see."

"Well now, you know we have something different to offer here." Carolyn said.

"Yeah, a longer drive." Colin replied, "I don't think people really care about the whole rural aspect as much anymore as compared to convenience."

Colin had extensive knowledge since he had covered stories of the short-term success that often turned into failure for local businesses. He was the columnist for the "Openings and Closings" section that was printed in the back pages of the Castwell Press News. It was a job he initially viewed as temporary after college. However, six years had quickly come and gone just as many other life changes and setbacks which had kept him stuck in a position in which he had very little interest.

Before closing the bathroom door, Colin said, "I just hope that this operation we run here doesn't end up in my section of the paper for the second time." He remembered writing about its grand opening a few years before.

Colin finished getting ready for work and went back in the room where he saw his mother standing near the kitchenette. Looking toward him, she asked, "Where to today?"

With his mind so caught up in Webster Inn's slow business, he had almost forgotten that the day he was about to begin had a much different appeal than most others.

"Actually." Colin said, perking up, "Not too far."

"An opening?" asked Carolyn.

"No." he replied as a bittersweet feeling took over, "A closing. It's Cleve's Corner."

Just saying the name filled Colin with memories and nostalgia that he knew would get him through the process of covering the story behind the business closing. It was a personal one that he already knew so well. He had actually been a part of it long before being assigned the story.

"Well, we all saw that one coming." Carolyn said, "Do you have time for breakfast?"

"I'd better grab something and go ahead. I need to go into the office first before I head back this way. But I'll see you a little later on."

Minutes later Colin was out the door and in his small car that had seen its better days. Those days were over a decade before when he had gotten the used car as a high schooler. The many miles he traveled on a daily basis throughout the county was one of the many reasons for the vehicle's wear and tear. Each day, after manually unlocking the door and putting his key into the ignition, Colin could only hope the engine would start. It had gotten to a point in recent days that there was no guarantee that it would. Some mornings required two or three tries while others required him to drive Carolyn's minivan which was not too far from having problems of its own. After Colin's attempt to start his car went smoothly, he took it as a good sign about the new day and was quickly on the highway in route to the Castwell Press office.

Colin entered the small office building that was located in the historic downtown area. He went straight to the morning staff meeting which he always dreaded. He was accustomed to the pressure that the boss commonly put on the staff as they gathered around her. Colin and the other staff members viewed it as meaningless. It had never intimidated him until the word "layoff" was thrown around more recently. The pressure had suddenly become real, as was the trepidation Colin felt going into his next story since he knew it could very well be his last. What put him at ease was the idea of going back into the small town that he believed to be the heart of the earth … Morriston.

Time immediately seemed to slow down when he took the highway exit and saw the vast acreage of pastoral landscape. He passed the large roadside *Webster Inn* sign. Less than a mile down the road, another sign read, "Welcome to Morriston." The building where he was headed was located just beyond the train tracks and the town's only stop light. "Cleve's Corner" was painted in faded letters on the white brick building. Like most everything else in Morriston, the building seemed immortal. It had never changed. Colin had several minutes to recollect thoughts of his times there as he waited for the arrival of the person he would interview ... Mr. Cleve's son. He was the present owner of the property but would soon be selling the place.

The atmosphere of Cleve's Corner provided Colin with memories of his very first visit there. It had been on a Saturday morning that his granddad Roy first took him to the store. Colin was just fine with waking up early on those weekend mornings to be with him. He even looked forward to it. He loved the delicious, all-you-can-eat breakfast food that was always available ... and the smell of freshly brewed coffee. What Colin came to find most worthwhile from those mornings were the long conversations between well-lived men who seemed to be solving the world's problems.

Colin had always marveled at his granddad and the other gentlemen as he listened to their conversations. When he was younger, he sat off to the side, trying to take it all in. As he got older, he became more involved in those conversations and went prepared with his own talking points each week. Never one to have friends of his own age to whom he could fully relate, Colin connected with that group in a way that he had always found difficult to do with anyone or anything else. That connection was what kept him going back by himself in the years after Roy passed on. Even as time passed and the group of gentlemen grew smaller, Colin remained a Saturday morning presence until the business closed. The operation came to a halt after the passing of the store's longtime owner, Mr. Cleve; and its doors were never opened for business again.

Since the building had become vacant, Colin dreaded passing by to see it empty. When he had occasion to drive by the abandoned store, he could not help but remember the height of its popularity. In those days, vehicles had surrounded the place and were randomly parked in whichever way the people went in and out the driveway. It was his dream to do something about the sight that saddened him. That dream seemed very far-fetched when he finally got around to asking Mr Cleve's son the big and final off-the-record question about the building's price tag.

With no financial standing to own the building himself in order to turn Cleve's Corner into a happening place again, all Colin could do was write the best possible article about it that he could. His goal for the article was to put together words that could capture the store's essence and atmosphere. His intent was to cause readers, regardless of how many or how few, to feel connected to the place in the same way he did.

Later that evening Colin sat at his small desk with the light from the dim lamp shining just brightly enough for him to see his notes from the interview. He reviewed them carefully, still feeling the essence of his visit earlier in the day. When he pulled out his laptop and was ready to begin typing, the rare burning desire that Colin felt inside replaced any pressure he had felt about the task of writing the article. With a newfound zeal, Colin began his journey expounding on the details of a story that he hoped would put him in a better position to further his career.

Chapter 4

Ring ...

Colin lifted his head from its resting position on his arms atop the wooden desk. He sat up to feel a painful strain in his back and neck.

Ring ...

He reached for his cell phone that had been placed directly beside his left eardrum, giving him the full effect of its ringtone. With the phone in his hand, Colin saw that the call that had awakened him was coming from the Castwell Press office number.

Rin-

"Hello?"

"Colin, good morning. This is Tina Smith."

Colin felt fully alert when he heard his boss's voice on the other end of the line. He quickly responded, "Oh! Hey there, Tina- Ms. Smith. How's it going?"

"Just fine. I came in a little earlier this morning and noticed your article was just submitted a few hours ago."

"Yes." Colin said as he checked the time to gain some perspective on how he had nearly pulled an all-nighter. "It was."

"Okay. Are you able to come in a little earlier to meet with me about it?"

"Uh-yes, of course. How early are we talking?" he asked.

"As soon as possible." she said.

"Sure. Yes, ma'am, I'll be on my way shortly."

When the brief phone call ended, Colin wondered what she had in mind. He had no clue as to what the mood of the meeting would be like. Based on the tone of his boss's voice, there was no indication of how she truly felt about the work he had submitted. He would just have to wait for the face-to-face meeting to find out. One-on-one conversations with his boss were not something that happened too often. Because of that, he felt that he was about to face either something really good or something horribly bad. For anything in between, he thought, she would have taken a "business as usual" approach … not a meeting.

Colin closed the laptop screen that had been blank since he had submitted the article. He placed it in his work bag. Soon, after doing just enough to quickly freshen himself up, he was out the door. His concern about the subject matter of the meeting grew during the drive to Castwell. Whether or not he did the Cleve's Corner story justice was something Colin had trouble recollecting. Stretching into the late night and early morning hours, the process of putting it together now seemed like a blur. The closer he got to the office, the more edgy his nerves became. When he arrived at the Castwell Press building, he took a moment to try to gather his thoughts and clear himself of the nervousness he felt.

Knowing that his boss was waiting on him, he didn't ponder long. He went to Tina Smith's office doing his best to look bright and confident.

"Ah." she said when he appeared, "There you are. Come on in."

"That was quick." Tina continued as Colin quietly took a seat in front of her desk.

"Well, I didn't want to keep a busy person like you waiting around for a guy like me." he said laughingly.

"You make a good point." she replied. "I am a busy person. Maybe too busy! Often that keeps me from interacting with, as you say, guys like you … other people like you, here at the office. You listen as I bark orders, and then you go and do your jobs. It's a cycle."

Colin replied, "I guess so."

"As the boss …" Tina began, "I sometimes feel like I don't truly know my employees, but after reading this …" Her voice, though it seemed cheerful enough, ebbed; and he couldn't help but wonder what was coming next. Then she held up a printed copy of Colin's article, "That's no longer the case with you."

"Yeah?" Colin replied, still uncertain as to what she meant by that statement.

"You wrote this piece with pure honesty and emotion. I was lost in your words and found myself right there inside Cleve's Corner. Even though I've never been before, your words made me feel like I was really there."

Colin responded with relief, "Oh, great. That was just what I hoped for." He felt a sense of relief as his doubt-filled question had been answered.

"This is much more than a story about a local small town business closing, and I don't want anybody to miss out on it. That's why I'm moving this article to the front page. Is that alright with you?"

Colin, in a genuinely surprised state, replied, "Are you sure? I mean ... Yes, of course it is. Wow."

"Colin, I'm definitely sure of it! Knowing the way this article impacted me, there is no question in my mind that it'll strike a special chord with the local people who have actually experienced Cleve's Corner themselves."

"Well, thank you so much for this opportunity. This is ... I just ... I can't really put it into words. Thank you." Colin said as he began to rise from his seat.

"Now wait a second." Tina said. "Before you go, there's another opportunity of which I want to make you aware."

Colin quickly settled back in the chair as he replied, "I'm listening."

"You're an alumnus of Morriston High, right?" Tina asked.

"Yes, ma'am. I am. Class of 2011."

"So I'm guessing you know of Mr. Jack Anderson, a longtime and well-beloved teacher there."

"Oh, Mr. Anderson? Yes, indeed I do. What a great guy. I was actually in his class. Junior year English. The best teacher I ever had."

"I see." Tina replied, "Even better. I'm sure you've heard that he's retiring after this school year."

"I did see something about that, yes." said Colin.

"Well, we want to run a story on him, and I've been trying to think of who could best handle that assignment. I believe your personal touch could really make a difference. Is that something you'd be interested in?"

"Most definitely!" Colin replied, "Without question!"

"Since the school year is winding down, I would like to go ahead and get this thing going. I'll make arrangements with the school for you to check with Mr. Anderson and set up an interview that works for both your schedules."

"Sounds good." Colin said with a smile.

"This is a big one." Tina said, adding her usual tone of pressure. "There are many people who feel connected to their former teachers. Teachers impact lives in a way that a corner store doesn't compare, especially someone who has taught as long as Mr. Anderson."

"Yes." Colin said in a much quieter tone, "Yes, I totally understand."

"Good. It's important to get this right." Tina said. Lifting the printed papers in her hand, she continued, "Just do whatever it is you did with this article. Go to that place and take everyone along with you."

"You can count on me." Colin smilingly responded as he stood to make his way out of the office of his boss and across the hall to his own work station.

Before Colin could really begin to feel any emotional ties to the new assignment, he first had to make a visit to Morriston High School. Having graduated ten years before, he had only seen the school in passing throughout the past decade. He had not even been inside since his final day as a student there. So he made an appointment to visit. He realized that some traditions had not changed as he waited at the door to be allowed to enter. He also noticed that the school's interior had not changed much at all. Neither had the people who were working in the office.

"You're here to see Mr. Anderson, right?" asked the school's secretary.

"Yes, Ma'am. I am."

"I'll let him know that you're here. He'll be coming down the main hallway."

Colin walked back to the hallway and looked down the corridor which was empty. He turned around to see a large bulletin board filled with flyers and information on the school's upcoming events. As he curiously began to scan the items posted on the board, there was one notice that really caught his eye. It was a flyer printed in bold letters. "MORRISTON HIGH SCHOOL CLASS OF 2011 TEN YEAR REUNION." Included on the flyer was information on the location … Morriston High School Gymnasium, the date of May 21st, and the time of 8:00 p.m.

Colin took another look down the hallway which was still vacant. He was trying not to show interest in the flyer about his class reunion. However, he could not resist taking another look at the reunion information.

Has it really been ten years? Colin thought to himself. Just then he heard the sound of whistling echoing from behind him.

"Well, I declare." Mr. Anderson said when Colin turned to face him, "It's Colin Webster!"

"Mr. Anderson! It's so good to see you." Colin said as he approached his former teacher with his hand held out, expecting a handshake.

"Put that hand away, Boy." said Mr. Anderson as he opened both arms for a hug.

Colin, not a fan of any kind of embrace, could not resist the quick hug from his former teacher who said, "It's been too long! How are you?"

"It has been." Colin replied, "I'm good. Congratulations on your upcoming retirement."

"I'd be lying if I said that I was counting down the days." said Mr. Anderson, "I'm surely gonna miss it, but I think it's time."

"I'd love to talk with you about that in more detail for an article I'll be writing for the Castwell Press."

"I remember how you were always a good writer. I'm really glad you pursued that. How would Saturday morning around ten o'clock work for you? We can meet at my place just outside of Morriston."

"That works fine for me." Colin said as Mr. Anderson pulled out a slip of paper and wrote down his address and cell phone number.

"See you then." he told Colin as they said their goodbyes, and he headed back down the hallway.

Colin walked back toward the main entrance. As he passed the front office, he heard someone calling his name before seeing another familiar face.

"Colin Webster?" she called to him. He knew that voice well. It was Ms. Tasha Wright, the school's media coordinator. He had spent a lot of time with her during his final semester as a library assistant.

Colin watched as she came from the cafeteria area carrying a paper plate. He laughingly responded, "That's me."

"You look like you just graduated last year! How long has it been?" she asked.

"Ten years, actually. It's hard to believe."

"I'm guessing you will be at the reunion here tomorrow evening?"

"Well." Colin said, "I'm not so sure if I will."

"Wait right here." Ms. Wright said as she walked to the front office. After sitting her plate of food down, she took a piece of paper off the front desk and walked it over to Colin.

"Take this." she said, handing over the same flyer he had seen on the bulletin board. "You think about it. It'll be fun! Everyone will want to see you."

Colin figured that was likely not true given that he had failed to keep up with his classmates over the years, but he smiled at her as he graciously accepted the flyer.

"I'll think about it." he said with every intention of doing the opposite. After a bit more chatting with her, he left the school.

When he arrived home later that day, he found his mother seemingly ecstatic.

"I have good news … great news!" Carolyn said when he entered their living space.

"Really? That's odd … because I do too." said Colin, "Something must be wrong, though. Such things don't often happen for us." he continued with a laugh as he placed his keys and the folded flyer on the nearby table.

"You first!" his mother said, insisting that he share the details.

"Two things." Colin said, taking a seat beside Carolyn, "One … my story about Cleve's Corner will be printed on the front page … the *front page*!!!! … and second …"

"Wait." Carolyn stopped him, "Of the entire newspaper?" she asked.

"Yes, the front page of the Castwell Press News. And that's not all …. I'll also be interviewing my … well, OUR former teacher, Mr. Jack Anderson, for his retirement story."

"Oh my ... how I love that man. He's the sweetest." Carolyn said. "Wow ... that's so great! I'm so proud of you for sticking it out. I knew your opportunity to do something different and fresh would come."

"Well ... what's new for you?" he asked her.

"This actually deals with both of us. I just got a call from four couples ... *four couples...*" Carolyn said, "who will be staying here tomorrow night. That means every room will be booked!!!"

"Every room? Wow! Including the master suite?" Colin asked.

"Yes, I was so surprised." she said, "The call came out of nowhere."

"So four couples just randomly called at the same time and requested the same night at the last minute?" he asked with some slight skepticism in his voice.

"I think they're all in town for some reunion. I believe they know each other, but still!!!" Carolyn said with great excitement in her voice.

"Oh, I gotcha. That makes sense." Colin responded making sure not to say anything more. He didn't want to say anything to dispel the pure joy he saw on his mother's face. He changed his clothes and went outside to continue work on a landscaping project on the property. Carolyn continued tidying up every room in preparation for the incoming guests. After she had finished, she still felt energized as she continued the cleaning process into her living area. With a duster in hand, she removed every item off of the tables. In doing so, she picked up the folded piece of paper that Colin had left behind. Naturally she had to unfold it, and on it she saw that it was an announcement. She read it silently ... *"Morriston High School Class of 2011: 10 Year Reunion"* ... *"Morriston High Gymnasium"* ... *"May 21ˢᵗ at 8:00 p.m."*

She refolded the paper and placed it back onto the table as if it had never been touched, but she knew she would have a hard time suppressing that information. It was nearing dinner time when a red faced and sweaty Colin came in after spending hours in the heat outside. Carolyn insisted that he shower before sitting down to eat.

He joined her at the table several minutes later and it was not long before Carolyn commented, "You know, I think I know why those couples will be in town."

"Oh yeah?" asked Colin before taking a sip of water.

"Morriston High School has a ten-year reunion tomorrow."

"Interesting." Colin said.

"Gosh, Colin! You know what I'm getting at. It's *your* class reunion. You'll probably know some of our guests."

"Maybe so. If they know me, just tell them I said hello."

"*Maybe you* should tell them … at the reunion."

"Mom, you know I'm not into that kind of stuff." Colin replied.

"Yes." Carolyn said, "I know … but just think of those days with your old buddies. Don't you think it'd be nice to see Cade, Trey, Reggie, Mary?"

"Mary?" Colin asked about his cousin, "Mary … You really think she would be there?"

"Well, you never know." Carolyn replied.

"I mean … she wasn't even at Grandma's funeral." Colin reminded his mother.

"I know … I know …."

"But do you think she would actually show up? She wouldn't … Would she?"

"Honey, I'm not sure. I was just naming your best friends from back then off the top of my head." Carolyn replied. She had no idea that the thought of seeing Mary would be stuck in his.

Shortly after dinner Colin retreated to his room to begin prepping for his big interview with Mr. Anderson. He took a seat at his desk and opened one of the drawers to search for a new yellow legal pad to list his interview questions. After removing everything in the crowded desk drawers and having no luck finding one, he began cramming it all back. It was then that Colin saw a small single sheet of notebook paper that he had thought was long gone. He picked it up and read it slowly to himself. He thought about the words and from whose lips they had been spoken. Tears came to Colin's eyes and slowly trickled down his cheeks as he remembered the moment, one of his last with his grandmother, when the words scribbled on the page were written. They were in his handwriting, but they came from grandmother Helen's mouth. The words read, "*Search begins where flowers bloom. Ends in a song sung. The keys lined up from old to young. Family together again."*

Colin closed the drawer with the note still in his hand. He kept it close by and within sight. The words at the bottom of the page, *"Family together again"* stood out most to him ... above everything else that was written. Colin wondered if that would ever happen ... if it was too much to ask for. As he started to lay the paper on the desk, he flipped it to the opposite side to see his Grandmother Helen's drawing there.

"The keys." Colin said quietly to himself as he took a close look at the drawing of three keyholes lined up vertically. "If only I had them."

Colin, remembering the poor state of mind his grandmother had been in when those words were spoken and the image was drawn, forced himself to believe everything on the page had to be directionless.

Speaking aloud, he said, "If only the keys existed." He tucked the paper under a paperweight off to the side and shifted into work mode.

Colin, not wanting to waste any more time, got up from the desk in hopes of finding a writing pad in the other room. After taking one step, his search was over when he saw his shoe on top of a blank sheet of paper that had been left lying on the floor. Instead of placing the single sheet of paper back in the drawer, Colin picked it up and put his pen to it.

One side of the paper was quickly filled and when it came time to flip it over to continue writing out interview questions, his plans instantly changed. What Colin saw on the other side of the paper took his mind to a place where he knew it could not afford to tread ... yet he would never be able to escape from it.

Chapter 5

Colin and Mary Webster's Bucket List (3-18-06)
(In no particular order)

1. *Be the star of a parade*
2. *Take our comedy routine to the stage*
3. *Find the end of a rainbow*
4. *TBD*

All it took was one glance at those words that had been written so long ago on the other side of the paper for Colin to remember the time and place they were written. It had been over fifteen years ago on a Friday afternoon. He and Mary had each enjoyed a Honey Bun and cold Diet Coke as they sat in their Grandmother Helen's walk-in pantry. It was the place to which the two twelve-year olds had usually retreated each Friday after a long week at school. With just enough space for the two cousins, the walk-in pantry was their spot to debrief and exchange thoughts on the latest middle school scuttlebutt. It was the place where their secrets were shared and many laughs were had … and on 3-18-06, their random goals had been determined.

Colin held the sheet of paper in his hand and could not help but chuckle aloud as he read over the list that he and Mary had begun to cobble together. He did not remember the reason behind any of the goals they had written down and realized that there most likely was none. Those details were not really important at all now. What did matter was the fact that, because of that paper, the decision about where he would be the next evening had become much easier for him to make.

Nearly twenty-four hours had passed when Colin found himself with the old bucket list in his hand once again. No part of his mind was any longer on what was on the other side of the paper … the side where he had written down talking points for his interview with Mr. Anderson. Though their meeting was scheduled for the following morning, he knew the possibility of another one happening that night was much more important to him. Once the final preparations for the incoming guests were complete, Colin bathed and got dressed for the big event with plenty of time to spare. As he placed what he deemed to be the perfect conversation starter with cousin Mary in his pocket, Colin heard the doorbell ring from downstairs.

"Could you run and get that? My hands are full at the moment." yelled Carolyn from the other room.

"No problem." Colin replied as he rushed downstairs to the front door.

Just before opening it, he remembered that these were most likely not ordinary stranger guests who had never seen him before. Instead, they would most likely be some of his old high school classmates who had *become* strangers. A sudden rush of embarrassment about the way they may perceive him rushed over him when he heard the doorbell ring once again. Pure relief came over him when he heard the sound of his mother's footsteps coming down the stairs.

Seeing him standing directly in front of the door, she asked him, "What are you doing, Son?"

Colin backed away and said nothing as he pointed to her and then toward the door before rushing past her on his way back upstairs. Carolyn did not quite know what to make of the characteristics of her son's crippling shyness. She had not seen that side of him since he was a young boy.

"I'm not here." Colin said to her from the upstairs landing.

"Uh … what?" Carolyn asked, before hearing the doorbell ring a third time, followed by a few knocks.

"Hey there, I'm so sorry about that." she said to the guests who were waiting on the porch when she opened the door. "Welcome to the Webster Inn. Come on in." she said with a smile to the eight people who were standing there with luggage in tow.

From the second floor landing, Colin looked out the window where he could see four cars parked along the driveway. He had not seen the guests, but he could hear their hearty laughs at Carolyn's welcoming wordplay as they came inside.

"Webster?" one of them said to Carolyn, "Wait a second, you're Colin's mom, right?"

"Yes. Yes, I am." Carolyn replied, "and you are?"

"It's me, Cade Baxter."

Colin's eyes widened when he heard one of his best friends from high school identifying himself to his mother.

Carolyn replied, "Cade! No way." She could still hardly recognize him after ten years and with a little additional weight.

"Yep. I'm sure you also remember Trey and Reggie over here."

"Oh my, yes!" said Carolyn, "I mentioned all three of you guys to Colin the other day."

"Good things I hope." Cade replied.

"For sure, I was trying to convince him to go to the reunion tonight, and I told him that I felt sure you guys would want to see him."

"It's been awhile." Trey mentioned, "I figure he's been busy changing the world or something like that."

Colin knew he was far from doing any such thing. Instead, he found himself crouched behind the corner on all fours while eavesdropping on the conversation below. Realizing how ridiculous he must look, Colin stood up and went back into the upstairs living area.

Reggie asked, "Is he going to the reunion?"

Carolyn, not aware of Colin's change of plans, replied, "You know, I'm not too sure about that." With a quick change of subject, she said, "But I don't want to make you guys late for it, so let me show you all to your rooms."

Carolyn did not recognize the other couple who was with Colin's old friends and asked them, "Did you guys also go to school with my son?"

"I did. My name is Bruce Williams. Colin and I weren't too close in school." said Bruce, whose large stature and deep voice took command of the room. Pointing to Cade, Trey and Reggie, he continued, "I really didn't start hanging out with these knuckleheads until we moved away and ended up in the same area."

"I'd like you to meet my fiancé here." Bruce continued as he pointed in her direction. "She's the oddball out … the only one of us who wasn't a Morriston High Wildcat. We're going to show her what we were all about back in the day."

Introducing her, Bruce said, "This is Amy. Come on over here … don't be shy, Amy. It'll be a long night of this." he said as he guided her over toward Carolyn.

"Hello." Amy said in a soft and timid tone that seemed to be in major contrast to Bruce's personality.

"So you guys all went to school together and are now married?" Carolyn asked the other couples.

"Yep. High school sweethearts, as they say." Cade replied as he leaned in to plant a kiss on his wife's forehead.

Like a flash in a dark room, Carolyn understood the disdain Colin had shown toward the idea of being with former classmates at the reunion. Gathering her thoughts, Carolyn quickly spoke up, "Oh … wow. That's great. Well, let me show you to your rooms. I know you'll want to rest and refresh a little before the big event."

After showing the guests to their rooms and doing a few more touch-ups in the parlor area, Carolyn went back upstairs to her living area to find Colin standing near the door.

"Have they left yet?" he asked.

"What has gotten into you?" Carolyn asked before noticing that he had changed into more formal attire. She added another question, "And where exactly are you going?"

"Nowhere until they leave."

"So you're telling me that you're actually going to the reunion tonight?" she asked.

"Yeah."

"You're going to a social gathering of these people but can't manage to open the door and welcome in some old friends?"

"There's more … look … I might as well just pop in for a bit." he replied, trying to downplay his sudden change of heart. With only one person in mind, he continued, "Just to see who all shows up."

Colin went back to his room to get his coat and car keys. After a short breather, he walked down the stairs that led to the garage. His car was parked in front of the garage door. He got into his car and began to back out of the driveway. He noticed that two of the cars in which the four couples had arrived were no longer there. He glanced at the clock on his dashboard and saw that it was already past the eight o'clock start time.

Like everything else in Morriston, the high school was only a few minutes away. When Colin arrived at the half-full parking lot, he made sure to park away from everyone else even though he figured that most everyone who would be attending had already arrived. Pulling up in his vehicle that differed greatly from many of the luxury SUVs that appeared to be well-suited for families put even more emphasis on just how far behind he was compared to his former classmates. That haunting feeling hung over him as he made his way into the gymnasium.

With the lights low and music playing loudly through the speakers, Colin looked out to see the gym floor full of couples dancing and people happily mingling with each other. He casually placed both hands in his pockets to feel the piece of paper that was the real reason for his attendance. Before Colin could use it to bridge the wide gap between himself and cousin Mary, he first needed to find her. As he began the tough task of trying to spot her among the crowd of people, he was approached by the event's planner, none other than Mrs. Tasha Wright.

"Colin Webster! I'm so glad you could make it!" She said to him, "Make sure you go over to get your name tag."

"Oh, no. That's okay." he replied. He really had no desire to have his name shown for everyone to see.

"Here." Mrs. Wright said as she grabbed his arm and walked him to the table, "Everyone has one."

When they got to the table it only took her a few seconds to pick his name tag out from the ones that were left.

"Here you go." Mrs. Wright said as she handed it over to him, "Now go have some fun!"

"Yeah, I'll try to." said Colin as Mrs. Wright walked away.

Before venturing away from the table to search for Mary, Colin took another look at the other name tags that were spread out. As he stuck his name tag onto the shirt that he wore, his eyes closely scanned the names. After seeing many that he hardly recognized, Colin spotted the one that ended his search for cousin Mary before it could begin. Seeing her name on one of the unclaimed name tags forced him to accept the fact that she was not there.

Of course she's not! Colin thought to himself, wondering why he had ever imagined that she might.

He quickly lost any desire to be there and turned in the direction of the exit. However, before he could take a step in that direction, the gym lights were turned back on one by one and the music stopped. Then he heard the sound that came from someone tapping on a microphone.

"Is this thing on? Can y'all hear me okay?" asked the voice.

Colin looked over to the center of the court where Mrs. Wright stood with the microphone in her hand as everyone made their way to the tables that surrounded the dance area.

"We're now going to begin our superlative event before enjoying the delicious catered meal that we have waiting." she announced.

Colin glanced over at the long tables lined up against one wall. Seeing the delicious looking food on them, he thought to himself that sticking around for that might not be such a bad idea after all.

Mrs. Wright continued, "Hopefully you all had a chance to look at our photo table to see your senior superlatives from back in the day. If not, I guess you'll just be surprised if your name is called. We will go through each superlative, and you will come up for a quick photo."

Colin, who stood off to the side near the catering staff, eased his way over to the photo table as Mrs. Wright began to call out the first superlative.

"For the 'most athletic' superlative ... Bruce Williams and Samantha Smith." said Mrs. Wright.

Bruce quickly stood up and stole the show as he began high fiving everyone in his path on his way to center court. The madness was just beginning, and it continued when he ripped off his shirt to expose the words "Morriston Wildcats" that were painted on his chest. Everyone watching got a kick out of the big reveal, especially his former classmates. They knew that Bruce's big personality had not changed much in the decade since high school. Colin noticed that one other person beside himself failed to laugh or even crack a smile at his antics. The other person was Bruce's fiancé, Amy. She knew it was the several drinks he had that brought out his comedic side, which never failed to turn into complete madness. Embarrassed by his antics, though they were well received at that moment by the crowd, Amy was desperate for some fresh air.

She stood and walked toward the gym's exit door. Colin, who was not amused by Bruce either, did not see her walk behind him as he had turned his attention to the photo table. As he continued to look at the superlative photos, Mrs. Wright said, "Okay! Wow ... thanks for that, Bruce. Let's continue on to our next superlative. For the 'dynamic duo' ... Colin Webster and Mary Webster!"

Colin did not budge as he stared at the very words that Mrs. Wright had just spoken into the microphone. They were under the yearbook senior superlative photo of he and Mary in what was thought to be the prime of their friendship. In reality it had been the beginning of the end, something that Colin became aware of much too late.

While he looked at the image of two people who appeared to be in control and on top of a world that they had created for themselves, Mrs. Wright asked, "Colin and Mary Webster? I know I just saw Colin."

Colin remained still as everyone began looking around in the awkward silence before Bruce stood up from his seat and yelled, "Well, you can count on me!" as he approached Mrs. Wright without noticing his fiancé's absence from the table.

"We're the dynamic duo now!" he said with an arm around Mrs. Wright. The room erupted in laughter again as the photographer captured their photo.

"Yes, okay. Let's move on to the next superlative." said Mrs. Wright as she tried to contain her laughter.

The moment she began to call the next set of names, Colin, with his head down, quickly made his way to one of the gym doors and pushed it open. He walked outside past a cloud of smoke that came from Amy's stress-induced cigarette. He was overcome with a numb feeling that blocked all of his senses. Without taking in the harsh smell or noticing her there in the courtyard, Colin's only concern was leaving and never coming back. He knew that he should have never returned in the first place.

Trying his best to escape, he first had to walk across the entire parking lot to his isolated car. Getting there was the first step of many that only people with thirteen-year old cars were forced to think about. When he turned the key in the ignition, nothing happened. Accustomed to the engine requiring a couple of tries, he turned the key a second time … and got the same result.

"Please! C'mon, not now." Colin said aloud to himself as he took the key out and put it back in for a third try. Turning the key again resulted in … nothing. Letting out a deep sigh, he came close to slamming his fist onto the dashboard. It was then he saw several dents which were the result of his having done that before in similar situations. So instead of that, he got control of his emotions, calmed down and pulled out his cell phone.

"Mom." he said after she answered, "I need a jump start to get home. I've got the cables with me. Can you bring the van?"

Carolyn replied, "You're coming home already?"

"Yes, I'm trying to."

"Isn't there anyone there who can help you?"

"Mom." Colin said, "Not exactly. At this point either you come or I walk."

"Okay, okay. I'll be right there."

Across the parking lot, Amy stood with her back against the brick building. She had totally ignored the large "No Smoking" sign posted above her. She had watched the random guy storm out of the gym with intrigue. There was something in each step he took across the parking lot that Amy thought was fascinating.

What's the story there? Amy wondered when she saw the man eventually get out of his car and open its hood. Her eyes remained fixed in his direction until she heard Bruce's voice from inside the building. Amy looked through the glass double doors to see him exiting the gym out into the foyer area.

"Ames?!" he yelled down the hall, even peeking his head in the women's bathroom as he repeated his nickname for her.

Amy quickly put out her cigarette and reached for her cellphone. With it up against her ear, she glanced over to the doors again to see Bruce making his way outside to the courtyard area where she was.

Without any reference to the phone call she pretended to be on, Bruce asked, "What's going on out here? It smells like crap."

Amy looked at him and pointed to the phone as she spoke into it, "Yeah, okay. Well I'll call you back. Alright."

Seeing the burnt out, flattened cigarette just beside her shoe, Bruce picked it up and threw it on her white shirt.

"Really?!" she furiously responded while trying to wipe the black ash stain off her shirt. The more she wiped, the more it spread.

"That's what you get. You know that's a no good habit."

"I don't think I'm the only one making unhealthy choices right now." she retorted.

"Don't sit out here and pout about it. C'mon." he said as he grabbed her arm, "Let's go back inside."

As he guided her toward the gym door, Amy looked back to the far corner of the parking lot to see the man getting some assistance. It was a sight that in some way gave her a sense of temporary peace ... assistance was something she needed. She knew that until help came, she was stranded ... clinging to the improbable hope that one day it would come.

Chapter 6

Colin was seated back at his desk. With pen in hand and a new legal pad in front of him, he tried to immerse himself in preparing for his big interview the next day. His laser-like focus was because of his procrastination. However, just as he got focused on what he should be doing, his attention was drawn to the sounds of the guests arriving back to the house. Hearing their voices as they stumbled inside, Colin felt sure that he knew what the rest of the night would entail. He had seen Amy's reaction several hours earlier as she watched her fiancé shift into party mode with his former classmates who still happened to be his friends.

When the car Amy was driving approached the "Webster Inn" sign, Amy knew there was no chance the group would be winding down any time soon. As she turned in the driveway with the headlights shining brightly in the night, she saw it. There was the car she had seen the man walk so passionately toward at the school. At the sight of the small car parked ahead in the driveway, she slammed on the brakes and came to a jerking stop.

"Woah! Easy there. What'd you see, a little turtle or something?" asked Bruce, who was seated in the front passenger seat. He turned to the couple in the back seat and said, "Amy isn't from around here, so she'll hit the brakes for just about any creature you can imagine."

Amy did not respond. As she continued to gaze ahead, Bruce waved his hand in front of her face while saying, "Hello? Ames? Let's go!"

She snapped out of the gaze that the sight of the car brought on and replied, "Right ... yeah." and then said the two most overused words in her vocabulary ... "I'm sorry."

Amy was the last of the group of eight to enter into the house. Instead of joining the others who were taking seats in the living room, she quietly went upstairs. She hoped she would not be missed by the group with whom she no longer felt comfortable. Her alone time was very brief since Bruce happened to see her walking up the stairs. Minutes later, when she did not join them, he excused himself from the group.

Amy heard the knock on the bedroom door that she had closed, and she knew exactly who it was.

"I'm getting dressed!" she said, only to see the door fling open.

"What's the matter?" asked Bruce as he entered the room.

"Nothing. Why?"

"Why? Because you're really embarrassing me by not being out there, Amy."

"Well, maybe I should just stay up here for the night." she replied.

"Fine by me." Bruce said as he left the room and slammed the door loud enough for Colin to hear it from his room.

Seconds later, Carolyn peaked her head in and asked him, "Colin, would you mind seeing what that was? I don't have the energy to deal with it."

Colin stood up from his desk chair and walked along the second floor hallway. He passed the first door on his left and noticed that it was closed. All others were open.

"Hello?" said Colin as he lightly knocked on the closed door.

Getting no response, Colin continued, "We kindly ask that you not slam the ..."

He stopped short when he heard another door from inside the room open and close loudly. Slowly he turned the doorknob and eased into the bedroom to see what was going on. In the quiet room, Colin first noticed a white shirt in the middle of the floor. He picked it up and saw a dark stain on it, only to drop it when he heard the sound of two flicks from the second floor balcony. He looked ahead through the thin curtain on the French doors to see the light of a cigarette between someone's two hands just as the person leaned against the railing and let out a puff of smoke.

Colin opened the balcony door with no reservations, and at the same time said, "I'm sorry … but we ask that you not smoke here."

A woman whose dark hair was blowing in the breeze turned toward him. Saying nothing, she took another draw on the cigarette and slowly blew the smoke out.

Colin watched as the smoke faded into the same direction that her hair was blowing. With still no response from her, he repeated himself, adding emphasis, "We *kindly* ask that you please not smoke here."

Her response came in the form of a blank expression on her shadowed face. Colin, seeing that there was no need to say more, continued, "If you promise not to slam any more doors, you may finish this one."

Amy, still saying not a word, recognized the man in front of her as the same one she had seen a few hours earlier outside of the gym at the reunion meeting. Her bleak, solemn mood over powered any normal reaction that she would have had from such a wild coincidence.

Colin leaned against the rail beside the women, but maintained his distance as he continued, "Because slamming doors can get pretty loud, you know?"

"Louder than those buffoons downstairs?" Amy asked.

"You make a good point. It is getting kind of crazy down there, but we're used to people noise around here." Colin replied as he remained by the rail and closer to Amy than she wanted him to be.

"Can I help you?" Amy asked, seeing the man was making himself quite comfortable in the space that she wanted to occupy alone.

Standing straight and backing away from the railing, Colin replied, "Oh, I'm sorry. This is just one of my favorite spots at the house. I used to stay in the room you'll be in tonight every time that I would come here … which was very often."

"So this was like home to you?"

"It still is!" Colin said as he walked back to the rail and placed both hands on it. "Just a much different version of it. One where, in your words not mine, buffoons can stay and leave a mess for my mom and I to clean up."

"I'm sorry … I apologize in advance." Amy said.

"So I'm guessing you're with that crowd?" asked Colin.

"Yeah. I guess when your fiancé wants to join his friends for a class reunion, you go."

"Fiancé? Congrats …"

Sensing he was waiting to hear her name, she replied, "I'm Amy."

"*Amy.* Got it." Colin said, "Congrats, Amy. Do you have a last name?"

"It's soon to be Williams." she said.

"What about *your* last name now? Not the one that you're about to take."

"Davis. Amy Davis."

"I can tell Amy Davis is *thrilled* to be engaged." Colin said with more than a little sarcasm evident in his voice.

Looking straight ahead, Amy replied, "When you've been engaged as long as I have, the thrill wears off. *But* we're set to start looking at venues soon, so hopefully we can get things going in that direction."

"It definitely could never be me. I don't know how you do it." Colin replied.

"Do what?" she asked.

"You know, the whole 'engaged to be married thing' and the 'married to be together for life' thing. Plus … your fiancé down there … that's a lot to deal with."

"So basically love and commitment? That's too much for you to handle?" asked Amy.

"I'm just saying it's not for everybody. Sometimes it does more harm than good, but most people never see it in that way."

"Someone's heart must be a little fragile." Amy replied, "Who hurt you?"

"Okay, look." said Colin, "Just finish destroying your lungs, take it easy on our doors, and enjoy your stay. That's all." he said as he made a quick entrance back into the room and closed the door behind him before making his way back to his own room for the night.

The next day, Colin arrived promptly at Mr. Anderson's house for the scheduled interview. There he saw a prime example of love and commitment in its truest form.

"Come on in." said Mr. Anderson, "I'll be right with you … make yourself at home."

With his yellow legal pad, ink pen and voice recorder in hand, Colin stood in the living room and looked at the framed pictures that took up the entire shelf space. Though all of the photos had the same style and background of a basic yearbook or graduation picture, the diversity was evident by the people in them … various races and genders were represented.

"Those are pretty neat, aren't they?" asked Mr. Anderson when he walked back into the living room.

Colin turned around to face him as he replied, "Yes, sir. They sure are … and I'm guessing you taught all of these people."

"Yep. These pictures range from over thirty years ago to this past year." said Mr. Anderson as he walked closer to the shelf.

"And they all just gave you their pictures?" asked Colin.

"Oh yeah, and this isn't even all of them."

"Wow." Colin replied, "Do you mind if I take a picture of them for the article?"

"Not at all." Mr. Anderson replied, "I know it seems like a bit much but, you know, my students, and really everyone at Morriston High, have always been my only version of family."

Mr. Anderson then opened the cabinet under the shelf and pointed out his collection of yearbooks from every year that he had taught there. He had them neatly lined up in chronological order.

He pulled out one and said, "For example, to me, this isn't just a collection of photos from one school year. It's a scrapbook filled with memories."

Mr. Anderson opened the yearbook to the first page and showed Colin all of the signatures and notes that had been written there.

With a smile on his face, he began to read some of them when Colin interrupted, "So how often do you look at all of these memories?"

"Well." Mr. Anderson said as he closed the yearbook and placed it back in the cabinet, "Whenever I'm not at the school trying to make some more of them."

"That probably was not that often. It seems like you were involved with everything imaginable at the school."

"You're right. I definitely spent more time in that school building than I did here at home."

"Was that intentional?" asked Colin.

"Hmmm…" Mr. Anderson mused as the expression on his face shifted to a more contemplative one, "Guess I never thought about it that deeply … but I'm sure part of it was intentional … yes."

While Colin wrote down some notes, Mr. Anderson continued, "A lot will change, that's for sure."

"What do you think your hardest adjustment to retirement will be?" asked Colin.

"Ah, I don't know. Probably what we were just talking about … letting go of the memories. The fact that reliving them will probably take the place of making new ones."

Though Colin felt a strong personal connection to that response, he did not let on. Instead, he knew he should shift the topic and change the mood of the interview to one that was less dismal. After glancing at his list of questions, Colin began to inquire further.

"What were-" he began as he looked up to see Mr. Anderson standing up from his seat. It was he who was about to ask the next question.

"What year did you graduate?"

"Uhm, 2011." Colin replied as Mr. Anderson was opening his cabinet door where he found the yearbook from that year.

He began flipping through the pages and stopped when Colin's senior portrait appeared.

"There he is!" he said, holding it up for Colin to see.

It was not his own picture that Colin focused on, but the one directly beside it.

"Yep, that's me." he said, wishing to get back to the interview that had gotten off track.

Colin realized the chances of that happening right away were not great when Mr. Anderson looked back in the yearbook and pointed to the same face that he had just seen in the other one just to the right of his own.

"Mary Webster … Your kinfolk!" Mr. Anderson said. "Boy, you two were a sight! What's she up to these days?" He obviously assumed that Colin would know.

"Ahem … uh … you know, a bit of this, a bit of that. Really staying busy." Colin replied as he looked toward the wall behind Mr Anderson.

Mr. Anderson sensed that his seemingly harmless question had struck an uncomfortable nerve with Colin, so he quickly changed the subject. He, of all people, knew the difficult complexities that can go along with family relationships. Though the interview continued and the planned questions were asked, Colin did not have much to show for it. When he sat down at his desk to recap the content he had gained during his time with Mr. Anderson, the inconsistency in the mood and theme of the conversation was exposed. The story that he really wanted to tell was not there. It was one that was simply unknown and nowhere to be found in answers to any of the questions that he had asked. Colin's doubts about his journalistic abilities had never been higher, and with the deadline for the assigned article quickly approaching, his concerns only heightened.

After staring at a blank screen while listening to a replay of his chat with Mr. Anderson, Colin finally decided to turn the audio recording off. He pushed his notes aside and pulled out his cellphone. He found the pictures that he had taken of Mr. Anderson's collection of student photos in his living room. Bits and pieces of inspiration began to spark even as Colin realized the difficult task of crafting a story out of what he saw. It would be his biggest challenge yet. To meet the deadline, he would have to piece it together very quickly and type profusely.

The first draft was nothing more than a brain dump as Colin cobbled together all the information he had collected. After making a little progress on the article, he found his thoughts constantly drifting and was continually having to bring them back to the assignment. He finally got up from his chair, wandered around the room for a few seconds and then stretched a big body stretch before sitting back down to continue. Settling back into his assignment, he eventually felt like he was making progress. The rhythm of his writing continually increased until he heard a sound that completely threw him off track.

Ding Dong

In that moment, he regretted that he had put a speaker to the doorbell in his room. He looked in the corner of his computer screen to see the time. It was a little late for any guests to be checking in, which was the reason he had felt the need for a doorbell speaker in the tucked-away second floor living area. When he saw the time, Colin realized that he had made enough progress to earn a brief snack break.

With a banana in hand, he came back to his desk to resume the work on the article. Colin pressed the return key to begin a new paragraph and took another bite of his banana. While he savored the sweet taste of the fruit, his hunger was satisfied; but his curiosity as to what was going on downstairs was not.

To justify extending his writing break, Colin decided, after tossing his banana peel into it, to take the trash down to the garbage can. As he walked down the stairway gripping the trash bag drawstring, he heard the sound of the doorbell again.

Ding Dong

After Colin stopped in confusion and turned his head to look around, he saw his mother coming from the kitchen.

"You haven't answered it yet?" Colin asked as she turned the corner and approached the front door.

"What do you mean?"

"That's the second time I've heard it."

"Are you sure? I've been in the kitchen for a few minutes and haven't heard a thing." she said.

"Yes, but it rang a few minutes ago. I thought you got it until I just heard it ring again. There was a big gap between the rings."

"Hmm." Carolyn replied, "Maybe that was just your brain telling you to give it a rest." before it sounded again.

Ding Dong

Colin stood still on the same step where he had stopped when he saw his mother. He wondered whether or not he had lost a piece of his mind in the process of writing. He watched Carolyn as she went to unlock the door and heard her voice after she opened it.

"Can I help you, Sir?" she asked, not recognizing the person who was standing on the front porch facing her.

Colin's curiosity growing, he walked down the stairs and positioned himself to throw the trash bag over his shoulder. Instead of it going over his shoulder as he had planned, he abruptly dropped the bag to the floor when he saw the man standing in front of his mother.

"Wh ... Why are you here?" Colin asked aloud, as he immediately recognized who it was.

Carolyn turned to Colin in hopes of gaining some insight about the man standing on their porch as she mouthed the question, "*Who is it?*"

"Go ahead." Colin said to the man, "Tell her who you are ... unless you're too ashamed."

"Carolyn." the man quietly said to her. "It's Nate. Nate-"

"*Brewer?*" Carolyn chimed in, "Nate Brewer??"

Chapter 7

Many years before …

"Is this a sure thing?" asked Eddie Brewer over the phone.

"Definitely." The other voice replied, "We're rich. Big time."

Eddie could only think of his marriage to Carolyn Webster as the occasion of their first wedding anniversary was soon to come. Even so, there was not much to celebrate in the mundane year that had lacked anything very special since they both said "I do."

To his business partner and friend on the other line, "This is great … really great. I'm getting out of this."

"Out of?"

"This downward spiral that's called marriage." Eddie replied

"I thought you wanted a part of that Webster fortune too?"

"I did, but there's too many ways that fortune will be divided up. It'll be messy … I can already tell. This deal is different … it has *my* name on it."

He saw the major investment deal in his latest business venture as the perfect opportunity for a fresh start that would not include his wife, Carolyn. Eddie wasted no time in making her aware of his decision. That evening their sons, step-brothers Nate Brewer and Colin Webster, sat with them through another dinner that lacked meaningful dialogue between any of them. Once the high school aged boys excused themselves from the table and went their separate ways, Eddie remained seated at the table. As Carolyn got up to begin clearing the table, he dropped the bombshell news.

"You know … I've been thinking … I want a divorce."

"Been thinking?" Carolyn echoed.

"Well, I've known ... I've known for a while now." Eddie told her, "Nate and I will be moving out of here in the next few days."

Just like that ... no explanations and no excuses. He had given Carolyn the news, and he

proved himself to be true to his word. He, along with his son, Nate, moved out of Morriston and separated themselves from the Webster family entirely. As the two of them enjoyed the riches that came with their new life, Carolyn was left with a deep emotional scar that took a very long time to heal. Colin was her main inspiration to move on.

Present day ...

Carolyn, realizing that it really was Nate Brewer standing just outside her door, sensed remnants of that painful night years ago when her husband had told her he was leaving.

"Wh ...Why ... I mean, what are you doing here?" she asked him.

Nate, with a painful look in his eye, explained, "Dad's gone." He lowered his head as he continued, "He's passed on."

Colin was quick to reply, "So you came here to open a wound that's already been healed?"

"Colin." Carolyn turned toward him to say, "Relax."

"No." Nate said, "I came to do my part in healing it. I've never agreed with my father's choices ... especially when it came to the way he left you guys. I hate that it took him dying for me to do this, but I just want to apologize."

"Okay." Colin said with his arm around his mother's waist. "Thanks for stopping by." he said as he reached for the door to close it. Carolyn put her hand on the door to stop him.

"Nate." she said, "For you to come here to tell me that shows your sincerity. Thank you for that. How are you doing with the loss of your father?"

"It was long overdue ... and honestly, it's been difficult to know I'll never get a chance to understand him. There's so many questions in my mind that are unanswered."

While Colin struggled to keep from rolling his eyes, Carolyn asked, "What brings you out to the area? I hope this wasn't the only reason!"

"No. I'm on a sales trip and was actually looking for a place to spend the night, but everything in this area seems to be booked. I saw the Webster Inn online. I suppose you guys are full as well." He paused briefly before continuing, "I didn't know whether you were still here or not, but I thought maybe someone here could tell me how to reach you." He paused briefly and smiled as he said, "Lo and behold, y'all are here!"

"Would you like something to eat or drink?" Carolyn asked.

"No, that's okay." Nate replied, "I better get going. It looks like I have a long drive ahead of me."

As Nate turned and began walking down the steps to go back to his car, Carolyn realized that she couldn't just let him just leave like that. She wanted to know more. She blurted out, "Wait a second, Nate."

When Nate turned around to face them again, Colin hopelessly closed his eyes. He knew what was coming next.

"You can stay here." Carolyn said to Nate.

Just as Colin expected, his mother's unwavering helpful heart and goodwill had overruled any bad memories that Nate's appearance might have brought to mind.

"But you're full, right?" he asked.

"Yes, mom." Colin added, "We are full! Remember?"

Carolyn, looking directly in Colin's eyes, replied, "We can make room for the night."

"You don't have to do that." Nate said.

"Yes." Colin said to his mother, "We *don't* have to do this."

Nate stammered, "I mean, I really shouldn't impose on you."

Colin pleaded, "He *really* shouldn't."

Nate continued, "But since you're offering ..."

Minutes later, after his persistence had been ignored, Colin found himself blowing up an air mattress in his room as Nate walked in carrying a large bag.

Once the pump was turned off, Nate spoke, "Quite the place you have up here."

Colin replied, "Quite the bag you have there." He was hoping the bag was not an indication of the length of time that he would be staying.

"Yeah." Nate said, "It's been a long sales trip. It's ending soon, thankfully."

"What is it that you're selling?" Colin inquired.

Nate, as if he had anticipated the question, was quick to respond, "Medical supplies."

"Oh yeah." Colin replied.

"What is it that you do?" Nate asked.

"Well I was, and should still be, doing my work for the article I'm writing on Mr. Jack Anderson. I'm a news reporter with the Castwell Press."

"Mr. Anderson?" Nate asked, "I was in his class during that school year when we lived down here."

"Yeah, I remember. ... Well, if you don't mind, I'm going to get back to work. My article is due in the morning."

"Sure, I'll get out of your hair. I'm going into town to get a bite to eat while you do that." Nate said as he walked out of the room.

When Colin opened his laptop it pained him to see what little progress he had made on his assignment. He knew he didn't have any time to waste, so he tried to clear his mind of the untimely appearance of his step-brother. Settling back into his work, the brief rhythm that he had before all the interruptions was long gone; and just as he was gaining momentum on the project, Carolyn knocked on his room door.

"Sorry to interrupt." she said, "But I think Nate needs your help."

Colin looked up from the screen and asked, "My help?"

"He just called from downtown Morriston and said his tire is flat and he's-"

Before she could finish, Colin closed his computer and stood up without saying a word. Carolyn could see the frustrated look on his face as she continued, "So can you check on him?"

As he headed toward the stairs that led to the garage, Colin responded, "Sure ... at this point, why not?"

"Don't you need to know where he is?" she asked.

As he continued down the stairs, Colin answered, "Morriston isn't that big, I think I'll be able to find him." He closed the door behind him before his mother had time to respond.

The darkened clouds in the sky above him were building and seemed to resemble Colin's irritated mood as he made his way into town. There, in front of the town hall, Nate had pulled over to the side of the street with a noticeable flat front right tire.

Nate opened the car door with his mouth full of food. In mid-chew, said, "There he is!"

When he saw Colin get the tools and spare tire from the trunk Nate told him, "You know, I've always wanted to learn how to do this."

Nate was in mid-sentence when Colin heard the first sound of thunder.

Colin quickly replied, "Well, now wouldn't be the best time to teach you." At first that did not stop Nate from standing outside to watch with a carton full of fries in one hand. However, it only took him feeling the first few raindrops on his skin for him to retreat back inside his car. In a matter of a few seconds, Colin found himself in a downpour with only half of the job done. He had already removed the flat tire, so he reached for the spare. He was already drenched to the skin, so he finished the job before he got back into his car dripping wet to head back home where the real work was waiting for him.

Once Colin showered and put on some dry clothes, he walked in his bedroom to find Nate sound asleep on the air mattress directly in front of his door. He stepped around the mattress and stumbled his way back to his desk chair. With his deadline less than two hours away, Colin read over what he had already typed and realized that the majority of it was no good. Holding down the backspace key, Colin took a brief dreary-eyed look over to Nate. Watching him breathe peacefully in and out, Colin wished to be in his own bed in the same sprawled-out position. He knew, though, that there was a lot of catching up for him to do before he could go to bed.

The next morning ...

Bzzzz ... Bzzzz

Colin opened one eye and felt the phone vibration against his left cheek that was pressed against the wooden desk. He lifted his head to feel the familiar strain in his neck. It was a feeling that occurred whenever he failed to make it to his bed after a night filled with a typing race against time. In a dazed state, Colin was not fully certain that he had even crossed the finish line on time. He could only hope so as he picked up his phone to see his boss's name on the screen ... yet another wake-up call that had beat his daily alarm.

He answered the phone without any attempt to hide his exhaustion, "Hello?"

"Colin, good morning. It's Tina Smith."

"Morning, Ms. Smith."

"Looks like you had another late night." Tina said, noting that his submission time was minutes before the midnight deadline.

"It was but I got it done, right?"

"Right. I actually want to talk to you about that ... would you mind coming to the office this morning?"

"Oh. On a Sunday?"

"That's today, isn't it?" Tina asked.

Colin stood up and replied, "I'm on my way."

He hung up the phone as he looked down at the air mattress and was reminded of Nate's random surprise visit. Seeing that he was no longer lying there, Colin got dressed with the thought ... and hope ... that Nate had already left and was gone for good. However, when he got downstairs, he found Nate "holding court" with the guests as they sat around the kitchen table. Though Colin managed to avoid Nate as he left the house, he could not help but think that he looked a little too comfortable for someone on the tail end of a long business trip.

Colin's thoughts were forced to shift as he drove Carolyn's van into the Castwell Press office parking lot and made his way inside. Upon entering the building, Colin greeted every staff member that he saw with a nod. As he walked across the bullpen, there was an awkwardness in the air of which only Colin was unaware. While the heads of staff members peeked out of cubicles and their eyes stared intently at Colin after he passed by, he looked ahead to see Tina Smith signal him in through her glass office window.

"Hi." she said, "Thanks for coming in."

"Of course. Was there any problem with my submission?" he asked.

"With the submission itself? No." Tina replied.

Before Colin could feel any relief, she continued, "The problems I have come from the content within the submission."

"Oh?"

"Look." she said, folding her arms on the desk, "This article was obviously rushed. Now I know you usually work best that way, but this one is something totally different from what we were originally hoping for."

Tina, noticing Colin's struggle to come up with a response, continued, "Your job is not at stake, but we need to go in a different direction with this story. I'm putting it in someone else's hands."

"Yeah ... No ... I understand that."

"I am reassigning you back to the "Openings and Closings" section of the paper. I have a big opening that I want you to start covering. It's a new wedding venue outside of Morriston. I know you'll do great with it."

While Tina wrote down the venue name and address on a slip of paper, Colin felt like a complete failure. His only thoughts were of how he had managed to come up short with the big opportunity he had been given. He could only blame himself for letting the numerous distractions affect his psyche. He knew that the events at home had caused him this set-back; yet, as Tina handed him the slip of paper, Colin was just grateful that he still had a job and that she had made this available for him.

"I want you to go ahead over there to set up times to interview the staff. Just put the last article behind you, Colin. This is a fresh start. Okay?"

"Okay. Thank you." Colin said as he took a look at the paper with "Harmony Acres" written on it ... his next destination.

He walked out of Tina's office to find the entire staff quickly leaving their post by her door after listening to the exchange. He was even more embarrassed as it became obvious to him that they had also gotten a glimpse at the less than stellar article for which he had been responsible. He managed to keep his pace and did not look back once.

Once in the van, Colin took a deep breath as it all sank in. However, he realized that he shouldn't be wasting time, so he typed the Harmony Acres venue address into his cell phone GPS. The destination came up on his screen, and Colin realized that it was off Highway 111 just past Morriston in an area he knew quite well.

Expecting to turn at any point along highway 111, he kept a close eye on the GPS directions. He soon saw a large roadside sign ahead just before hearing, "Your destination is to your right." Colin slowed down and nearly came to a complete stop on the highway as he gazed in the direction of the large arrow on the "Harmony Acres" sign. The narrow dirt road that separated two fields of corn was one of many in the area, but Colin could immediately recognize this one. It was one that he had turned down many times before in his younger years.

Colin drove slowly down the road, taking in the scenery surrounding him. This property had once been owned by his granddad, Roy Webster. He looked at the acres of pine trees in the distance and could not help but think of the opportunities that could have come by farming them as his granddad once had. It was apparent and came as no surprise that his uncle, Tony, who had inherited that particular piece of land, had different plans when he had let go of the place.

As Colin increased his speed a little, he saw another sign ahead of him through the small space through the trees. To himself, Colin repeated the words that Granddad Roy would always say when he approached the crossroads in the wooded pathway, "Right, left, right."

Even if those words had been forgotten and the directions were foggy for Colin, he would have been just fine with the assistance of three signs posted with red arrows ... one pointing to the right, the next to the left, and then another right. When Colin made the final right turn, what he saw in front of him was unrecognizable.

"Oh my." Colin said as he passed yet another directional sign with the words "Harmony Acres" posted on it. Though the lake and original cottage where he had spent countless nights was still in front of him, there was no denying the commercialization that came with the additions. There were now additional buildings ... a chapel, restrooms, several smaller cabins ... and official parking spaces.

Colin parked the van near the restroom area. He got out and momentarily surveyed the area before he began walking toward the newer cabin which had an "Office" sign posted beside the front door. While doing so, he took in the same fresh air and the aroma he remembered from the countless family summer get-togethers he had enjoyed there during his early youth. He looked out over the lake and visualized how it had looked then. It was as if every other building surrounding it, aside from the original cottage, suddenly disappeared. That moment allowed him to picture in his mind how the area once had been and how he felt it should still be.

That scene faded when Colin nearly bumped into the wooden post in front of the office building. Pulling his thoughts together, he entered the building and saw a young lady at the front desk.

"Welcome to Harmony Acres." she said as she welcomed him with a smile, "May I help you?"

Colin pulled out his Castwell Press badge, held it in front of her and replied, "I'm here to schedule an interview with someone from your staff. We are to do a feature on your opening."

"Oh, sure. She's actually finishing up a call right now. If you don't mind waiting, it shouldn't take too much longer. I'll let her know you're here."

Colin gave a thumbs up and walked back outside to wait. The memories continued to flow as what he was seeing reminded him of his times at the family lake compound. A great deal of detail … certain moments, faces, and even voices … came to mind as if they had just occurred. One specific voice … the one of his favorite cousin, Mary, seemed to sound as if it was coming from directly behind him.

"Hello, Sir." said the voice in her exact tone.

As he stood there with his thoughts still lost in the midst of a different time, Colin heard the voice. Before he turned to respond, he briefly thought about how many times he had heard that voice and figured that it should not surprise him that just being in the setting would cause most any female voice to remind him of hers. Still caught up in his revisit to his past, he slowly began to turn toward the person whose voice he had heard. When he looked at her face, he could not believe his eyes. Instantly they were locked with those of the person he had so longed to see. Was she standing right before him? Was it indeed the voice of his favorite cousin, Mary, standing there waiting for his response?

Chapter 8

He frantically began an internal conversation with himself, *That's her. No …
it can't be. It's all in my head. Are you sure?*

"It's me." she said, "Mary."

Realizing that the lady who had appeared before him was not just a
figment of his imagination, Colin instantly sobered up from his intoxicating
thoughts.

"Okay! Okay!" He muttered. "I'm just messing with you." said Colin in
an attempt to normalize the moment.

"Oh, right." Mary said with nervous laughter.

"You know, because … it's been so long. It's the 'who are you, stranger?'
bit."

"I see." Mary said before a few seemingly long seconds of uncomfortable
silence followed. "So …" she said, knowing her time was too precious to be
wasted, "What are you doing here? Scouting your wedding venue?" she asked.

"Most definitely not." Colin replied before he could finally recall the
actual reason, "No, I'm just here to schedule an interview about the place.
Would you know something about that?"

"Credentials?" she asked.

"I'm sorry?" he stammered as he fumbled to find his badge.

"Are you with a statewide paper or …?"

"Oh, no. Just local … the Castwell Press." Colin replied as he pulled the
badge from his pants pocket.

Mary thought for a second and replied, "Well, I'd usually just let someone else from the staff handle this; but since we have a prior connection, I'll answer a few questions for you tomorrow morning at nine o'clock. Does that sound good?"

Prior connection? Colin thought to himself, *Really?* Knowing of nothing else to do but just go with the flow, he replied, "That'll work. Thanks."

As she looked over her shoulder to see some staff members approaching her, Mary said, "Great. I'll see you tomorrow." while backing away to join them.

"See you … then." Colin said.

He stood still and watched Mary converse with the hectic workers. One of them held a clipboard with something for her to look at and give her approval. As Colin watched her point the staff in different directions, he knew that the person he had just encountered was a far cry from the one to whom he had once been so close. Though they were physically closer than they had been in many years, Colin felt as if many more miles had just been added between them. He slowly made his way back to the van, got in and sat there thinking of what had just taken place. On the drive back home, he couldn't help but dwell on how different this encounter had been from what he had, through the years, imagined it would be.

Colin went through the garage and up the stairs that led straight to his room when he arrived back home. The already challenging task of interview prep was taken to another level now, especially since his confidence in finding the right questions was still shaken from the past assignment. With his chin resting on his left hand, Colin felt the cellphone in his pants pocket vibrate and was quick to answer the call from an unfamiliar number.

"Hello?"

"Colin, this is Jack Anderson."

"Mr. Anderson!" Colin said, "How's it going?"

"Good. I was just contacted about meeting someone else for another interview for that article. I'm sorry things didn't work out for you to go forward with it. I should have given you more to work with. It's my fault."

"No. No, that's alright, Sir. I was not on my A-game, but everything will work out just fine." Colin replied.

"Well, I still feel like I owe you one, and I want you to come by the house sometime. I found something in my teaching memorabilia that I think you will thoroughly enjoy."

"That's very kind of you." said Colin, "I will try to make my way over there at some point tomorrow."

After hanging up the phone, Colin found a reason to delay the prep work for his new assignment. He knew that there was no use trying to begin work with an empty stomach. Leaving his room, he was making his way into the kitchenette when he saw Nate.

"There you are, what's up?" Nate said to Colin when he heard him enter.

Colin noticed the stains on Nate's shirt and the sweat on his skin and asked, "What are you doing?"

"Don't worry, I'm not eating all of your snacks. I just needed to refuel."

"For what?" asked Colin.

"Well, since you've been so busy with work, your mom didn't want to bother you with the jobs around here. This morning I offered to help out, and it turned into a full day's work."

"Oh, yeah?" said Colin as Carolyn walked in to join them. "Hey, darling." she said to him, "I didn't know you were back."

"Yep. I'm here ... and so is Nate."

"Isn't it so nice for him to help out? He even offered to stay another night to finish the work we started." she said.

"Oh, he did?" Colin asked as he looked over to Nate, "I thought he'd want to be heading home now ... you know after a long 'sales' trip."

"Okay, look." Nate said, "I mentioned this to your mom earlier, but home was not exactly somewhere I was ready to head back to today. I just needed a couple of extra days, but I promise that I will leave tomorrow morning and be out of your way."

Knowing that it was officially the final night of having to share his room with Nate, Colin felt a little more acceptant of the situation. Back in his room that night, though, the nonstop chatter from Nate hindered Colin as he tried to get work done for the next day's interview. Once it seemed as if Nate had finally gone to sleep, there was still another question he had been saving.

"Hey, Colin."

Colin let out a deep breath and, without moving his eyes from the laptop screen, replied, "Yes?"

"Do you ever go up to Lake Webster at all?"

Colin abruptly stopped typing and paused briefly before replying, "It's more like Lake Wedding now … but I actually went there for the first time in years yesterday."

"Yeah? Man, that was quite the place!" said Nate.

"You remember it?"

"How could I forget? That one summer was the best."

"Yeah, it's changed a lot. I'll be back there tomorrow for this interview I'm trying to get ready for now."

Nate quietly replied, "Good to know."

Unable to clearly understand what he had said, Colin asked, "What's that?"

"It's good to know that because … well, now I'll stop blabbering on and get to sleep."

Just when the noise had ceased around Colin, more came from the downstairs area that Carolyn heard very clearly from her bedroom. What kept her from getting up after hearing the sudden sound of glass breaking was the silence that followed. She determined that a guest had dropped something and dismissed it from her mind, allowing her to sleep good enough to forget it even happened. Carolyn was reminded of it early the next morning though when she walked downstairs to find pieces of a broken vase piled on the floor. On top of the pile was a wad of cash and a note from the guest responsible for the damage. Though Carolyn saw the gesture as a generous one, she knew there was no amount of money that could replace the priceless vase that had been passed down from her parents.

Getting down on her hands and knees to clean up the glass from the floor, she found herself looking up at the other vase on the counter. It was of much less value than the one that had been broken. Carolyn disparagingly said to herself, "*Of course it was this one.*"

She gathered a few of the larger broken pieces thinking to keep them once she had disposed of the smaller pieces and slivers of glass. It was then that she noticed another piece unlike any of the others. She instantly put down the pieces she had already collected in her hand, and picked up the unusual one. With her long nails, she peeled off a few layers of duct tape to find a small key that had been stuck to the inside of the vase. Carolyn knew that if any piece should be preserved it was that one. With a busy morning ahead and needing to get going, she taped the key back to the broken piece and placed it in her purse along with the wad of cash the guest had left behind. Trying to be as quiet as possible, Carolyn pushed the pile aside and left it behind to clean up later. She hurried out to the store so she would be back in time to prepare breakfast for the Webster Inn guests.

Soon after Carolyn left, Colin's day started as he woke up to find Nate still asleep on the air mattress. As soon as Colin went to the living area's bathroom, Nate opened both of his eyes. He quickly stood up and prepared to get dressed while letting the air mattress deflate.

When Colin got back from the bathroom, he found Nate folding up the air mattress. Surprised that Nate was awake and up, he said, "That was quick."

"Yeah, I need to be on my way." Nate replied as he put his bag over his shoulder.

"Same here." Colin said as he reached for his work bag.

Nate followed Colin down the garage stairs. "Thank you for giving me a place to stay. I really appreciate it." Nate said as he reached out to shake hands with Colin.

"Don't thank me, thank mom. But it was no problem after all."

When Colin walked outside to see that Carolyn's van was gone, he continued, "Speaking of mom, where is she?"

"Oh." Nate said, "She mentioned last night something about running to the store early this morning."

Nate had heard of Colin's car troubles from Carolyn and watched as he worriedly checked the time.

Colin asked, "Did she say when she'd be back?"

"I'm not sure." Nate replied and then asked, "Why? Do you need a ride today?"

"I hope not." Colin replied as he approached his car and got in to try to start it.

After a few failed attempts, Colin sat there and contemplated rescheduling the interview with Mary. Just before dialing the number, Colin realized the time crunch he was in to produce promising content for the Castwell Press. He let out a deep sigh, got out of his car and looked at Nate who had happily waited off to the side. He answered Nate's question by nodding his head slowly.

"Perfect." Nate said.

"What?" asked Colin.

"You know." Nate replied, "It's perfect that I am still here to give you a ride to the Lake … right?"

"Right."

Colin sat in the passenger seat of Nate's car and guided him from the Webster Homestead to the lake property.

"Harmony Acres? How romantic." said Nate as they approached the sign and turned onto the long dirt road.

"Tell me about it!!" Colin sarcastically replied.

After making the three turns in the wooded area, they reached the opening. Parking in front of the office cabin, Nate asked Colin as he got out of the car, "Will this take long?"

Colin replied, "I have a feeling that my time with the boss lady is limited, so probably not."

"Okay. I'll just probably look around while I wait." Nate said as Colin walked toward the office door.

When Colin entered the office, he saw his cousin, Mary, busy at work. She was on the phone, and with her staff members around her, she hardly noticed when he rang the front desk bell to let them know he was there.

Mary briefly looked up to ask, "Is it nine already?" then checking to see it was minutes past nine, she continued, "Now we're behind schedule."

As she stood up, Mary told her staff, "I have to do a quick favor. I'll have my walkie talkie on me, so let me know when they get here."

Favor? Colin thought as she approached him. He smiled and asked, "Busy morning?"

"We have our first couple coming to tour the place this morning. Why don't we do that too? I'll show you around."

"I guess you have had a busy morning too." Mary said as they walked away from the office.

"What makes you think that?" he asked.

"Well, you were a little late."

"Oh, I had some car troubles and-"

"No-no. Let's not dwell on it and waste any more time."

But you brought it up? Colin thought, but instead of saying that, he asked, "Do you mind if I take some pictures?"

"You're the photographer too?"

"I don't know if that's what you'd call someone who takes pictures with this." he replied as he held up his cellphone.

"Sure, I don't mind." she said, while thinking he must be part of a low budget operation.

After snapping a few pictures of the venue's exterior, Colin looked over to the original cottage and asked, "Do you mind if we go in there? It's been so long."

Mary replied, "Nothing has really changed inside. We haven't even touched anything in there just yet."

Colin, thinking any semblance of what the property used to be had been erased, grew more intrigued and replied, "Even better."

After leaving the car just after Colin had entered the office cabin, Nate had made a b-line to the original cottage. Once he made his way in through the door that, to his surprise, was unlocked, Nate stopped when he heard the sound of voices from outside. He looked out the nearby window to see Colin and Mary walking directly toward the cottage. Nate quickly made his exit after finding the back door and managing to close it behind him seconds before they entered the front one.

Mary flipped on the light switch, and immediately Colin took in the same look and absorbed the same aroma from every item that had not been moved an inch since his last visit. Feeling as if he had entered a time capsule, Colin could not contain his amazement. "You were right, this is incredible." he said as he stood there in awe.

"We're planning to remodel the whole place into suites for the guests eventually … maybe even a bed and breakfast. We'll see."

"Wait. What? We have one just a few miles from-" Colin said before being interrupted by Mary's phone ringing. That stopped her from sharing anything more about the future plans.

"Excuse me." Mary told him, "I have to take this call."

When she stepped outside to answer the phone, Colin looked over to the dark hallway that was to the right of the foyer. He used his cell phone flashlight to find the hall's light switch. Once the hall light was on, his eyes immediately went to the last door on the left. Colin walked toward it. He paid no attention to the other rooms where the adults in the family had retreated to sleep after a long day on the lake. The door that he was about to open would take him into a space where the priorities were much different for those occupying it.

Colin walked in and took a seat on the bottom level of one of the three bunk beds in the room. Seated there, he so vividly remembered the endless array of fun and laughter with his cousins. He recalled the competitive board games and their faking sleep when a tired parent would come knocking on the door late into the night.

Remembering that Mary had said, and now seeing for himself, that nothing in the cottage had been touched in years, Colin thought it would not hurt to leave with a keepsake. He stood up from the bunk bed and casually reached for the closet door handle to open it. Colin did so in a way that made what came next even more of a shocking surprise. Instead of seeing the expected stack of board games and extra bed sheets, he was surprised to see numerous miscellaneous items that had been crammed in the closet come tumbling out. The mess that was made from everything that had been leaning against the closet door exposed something else hidden deep in the corner of the closet.

"What do we have here?" Colin asked himself, as he didn't remember ever seeing the storage trunk before.

He figured that if there was a keepsake worth having, it would most definitely be in there. When he kicked the items that had crashed to the floor aside, Colin dragged the trunk toward him and found that either the items within it or the trunk itself was quite heavy.

It took both hands to pull it toward him; and just as he grabbed hold of the trunk, he jumped when he heard Mary's voice from behind him asking, "Need help finding anything?"

Colin bent down again, flipped the three silver knobs up, and lifted the handle that had kept the trunk closed. Mary stood behind Colin as he opened the lid. Each of them had a very different reaction to the three vertically aligned key holes what appeared before them. What Mary saw as a dead end, Colin saw as something entirely different.

Chapter 9

Colin immediately gained a new perspective on the sketch his Grandmother Helen had given him. What he was looking at in the trunk was nearly identical to what she had drawn on the sheet of paper.

"That's a shame." Mary said, "Oh well."

"Yeah, it sure is. You know what? I think I might take it with me so I can have another try at finding a way to open it somehow."

"Wait a second." Mary told him as he began to pick up the trunk, "What do you know?"

"What do you mean?" he asked.

"I think there's a reason why you would want to take it." she said.

"Yeah, to try and open it. Don't you want me to?"

"No, it's fine. Why not just put it back and clean all this stuff up? Unless you actually have a way to unlock it ... do you?"

She's good ... Colin thought to himself before replying, "There may be a way."

"I'm running short on time, but I'll make a deal with you." Mary said, "If we move this interview back a day or two, you can take the trunk with you and do whatever it is you need to do. I don't want you to explain how you think you could open it until you actually know you can."

Despite running short on time himself, Colin replied without hesitation, "Okay. I can do that."

Colin carried the trunk out of the cottage and headed toward the car where Nate waited with his back leaned up against it. Nate was talking on the phone when he saw Colin approaching and said, "I've got to go, but I think you'll be hearing back from me soon."

As Colin got closer, Nate saw the look of struggle on his face as he carried the trunk and asked, "Need a hand?"

"No, that's fine. Would you mind opening your car door?" Colin replied.

"Sure thing." said Nate as he opened the back door and asked, "What's all this?"

"Well." Colin said, feeling relief when he placed the trunk in the backseat. Closing the car door, he was determined to keep the potential value of it under wraps, "Just some old family stuff."

"I see. So we're done here?" asked Nate.

"Yep." Colin replied, "We can head out."

As they were leaving the Harmony Acres venue and making the first turn down the wooded pathway, they noticed another car coming toward them, moving slowly toward the entrance. In all of Colin's experiences of coming to and from the lake, he had never before met another vehicle on the path.

"Watch out for this traffic ahead." Colin told Nate, unsure if the two cars could successfully pass each other in the narrow wooded area.

Nate continued to ease forward, as did the other vehicle. When they met, it appeared there would be only a few inches to spare between the two smaller compact cars.

"Like a glove." Nate said as they successfully managed to avoid hitting the other car or any of the surrounding trees.

"A tight glove." Colin replied, giving the other driver a wave, "That must be the couple coming to visit."

When Colin pulled out his cellphone to make his boss aware of the slight interview delay, he saw a message on the screen that Mr. Anderson had sent nearly an hour earlier.

It read, *I am home all morning. Stop by at any time that is most convenient for you.*

"Crap!" Colin said aloud, "I almost forgot."

"What's that?" Nate asked.

"I was supposed to stop by Mr. Jack Anderson's house at some point this morning. I'll get mom's van and go. Just head to the Webster Inn."

"No, that's okay!" said Nate, "I'll be happy to drive over there. Just tell me where to go."

"Trust me." Colin replied, "You've done enough. I don't want to hold you back from leaving any longer."

"I insist." Nate told Colin.

"Well, since we're already out this way, I guess that's fine."

As they reached the end of the dirt road and were about to turn onto highway 111, Colin gave Nate the go ahead with directions to Mr. Anderson's. He scrolled through his contacts to give his boss, Tina Smith, a call. Just before pressing her name, he received a call from his mother.

"Morning, Mom." he answered.

"Where are you?" Carolyn asked.

"Leaving the venue and stopping by Mr. Anderson's place before heading back home."

"How did you get over there?"

"Nate's driving me."

"Perfect." she replied. "He's been a big help, and I wanted to invite him to have dinner with us before he leaves."

"I don't know if he could do that, I think he really has to go soon."

"Well I'd at least like you to offer or just pass the phone over and I will." Carolyn said.

"Everything good?" asked Nate.

Colin said nothing as he held the phone out for him to take.

"Hello?" asked Nate with Colin's phone in one hand as the other gripped the steering wheel.

Colin gazed out the window at the passing fields while he listened to the quick exchange over the phone.

He knew the dinner was a done deal when he heard Nate say, "You know? I think I could possibly do that. Yeah … that'd be great. Thanks for thinking of me!"

Nate handed the phone back to Colin, who gave him the final piece of direction before reaching Mr. Anderson's house.

"You'll need to turn down this road here."

After passing a few houses, Nate turned in the driveway as Colin pointed and said, "This one to the right."

When the car came to a stop, Colin unbuckled his seat belt and asked, "Do you want to come in and see him?"

"No ... that's okay." Nate replied, "I'll just wait out here. You said it wouldn't take too long, right?"

"It shouldn't. I'll try not to let him talk too much." Colin said as he got out of the car and headed toward the house.

Nate glanced in his rear view mirror to see the trunk sitting in the backseat after Colin had been let inside Mr. Anderson's home. That was the official sign that, thanks to a few lucky breaks along the way, a plan had successfully unfolded. With the ultimate prize in his possession, Nate shifted the gear into reverse and backed the car out of the driveway. He then called back the person to whom he had been speaking earlier when he saw Colin with the trunk. Before speeding away there were only three words that Nate needed to say over the phone before hanging up once again ... "I have it."

Inside Mr. Anderson's home, Colin sat on the edge of the living room sofa knowing nothing of Nate's escape. Instead, he was listening to Mr. Anderson while, at the same time, looking at the box on the coffee table that had his name written on it.

"I ran across something when I was cleaning out my attic the other day, and I immediately thought of you." Mr. Anderson said.

He pulled out an old typewriter from the box and held it up. "This is a Smith Corona typewriter. It was gifted to me, and I got a bit of use out of it in my early teaching years. I wanted you to have it." he said.

"Are you sure? Why me?" asked Colin.

"I don't know if you'll ever get any use out of it. I'm sure it needs a lot of repairs, but I want it to serve as a reminder for you to never stop writing ... no matter what."

Minutes later, with the typewriter safely in the box, Colin started out of Mr. Anderson's house as they said their goodbyes.

"We'll keep in touch." he said to his former teacher as he made his way to the door.

Mr. Anderson opened the door and looked out to the driveway. Only seeing his car there, he asked, "What are you driving?"

"Oh, uh …" Colin started to answer him just as he walked out and turned to see no sign of Nate's car anywhere. "What the …?"

Nate was already nearing the new place he called home by the time Colin noticed his escape. It was a small mobile home located several minutes outside of Morriston. When he pulled up to it, he parked closely beside another car which was owned by the person with whom he shared the mobile home. Nate, carrying the trunk, squeezed his way between the cars and pushed the door open. "I'm home, Dad!" he called.

Dad, as in Eddie Brewer. He was, in fact, alive but not doing so well. The business that had promised to be his fast track to riches had gone downhill very quickly. What he had once used as the ticket out of his brief marriage to Carolyn Webster was no longer existent. Eddie's failures had often reminded him of the day that his big ideas of personal success had allowed him to push aside what was like a bird in his hand. He had always wondered what it would have been like if he hadn't left the Webster clan.

What Nate had in his hands might just be the answer. The moment he took hold of the trunk, he felt like the solution to his problems would be perfectly executed. It was not until he opened the trunk to find the three key holes that he realized the solution might not be as easy as he had imagined.

"What's this?" he asked his son.

Nate looked to see what he was pointing to, but he had no answer. The look on his father's face caused him to take a closer look. After examining the areas around the three key holes, he had no answer to the question.

"What IS this?" his father asked again more forcefully.

"I'm not sure! I hadn't opened it yet to see that."

"Your job is to find this stuff … and to not show up here with a half-done job!!"

"So what do you want me to do?" Nate asked.

"I want you to go back where you got it and find some answers … or find three keys to open this thing up. Take this trunk with you, act as if you think nothing special of it."

"So you expect me just to show up again?"

"You did it once; you can do it again" Eddie firmly said.

"How do I explain myself?" Nate asked.

"How do I know? Something … anything … you figure it out; and while you're at it, take the key copier kit with you just in case. We'll eventually need three of them in our possession, either way."

Meanwhile …

"And now we need three of them." Colin said to Mr. Anderson as they turned into the driveway at Webster Inn. Mr. Anderson had been kind enough to give him a ride home when they discovered that Nate had disappeared. During the entire ride, Colin had been explaining to him everything about the trunk.

"Now, tell me again, what was that line your grandmother wrote down?" he asked Colin.

"Family together again." Colin replied.

"That's beautiful … it really is." Mr. Anderson replied, "And whatever is in the trunk could do just that?"

"Who knows … maybe. Guess I'll never know. I'm sure it's long gone now, but even the slightest chance of our family being together again gave me so much hope."

"Never lose that hope, Colin." Mr. Anderson replied, "Hold onto it tightly."

As Colin started to get out of the car, Mr. Anderson kept talking. Speaking from his own experiences, he continued, "Listen to what I say, Colin … don't neglect the family within reach while you're pursuing those who are far away."

After Colin had thanked him for the ride and bid him goodbye, he headed toward the Inn. He knew his mother would be there to greet him. She was always within reach. How to share this latest dilemma with her, he was not sure.

"Don't you see?" Colin asked her after explaining how Nate had fled off with the trunk, "We never should have trusted him."

Her mind still trying to absorb all Colin had told her, she seemed to not even hear what he had said about Nate. "Three key holes?" she asked.

"Yes. Why?"

"Well, today I-"

Ding dong

Sensing that his mother had something important that she was about to share, Colin did his best to ignore the doorbell speaker that had stopped her mid-sentence.

"Today you?" he asked just as the doorbell sounded again.

Ding dong

The two of them made their way to the front door and opened it to find Nate Brewer waiting on the porch. Just in time for dinner, he acted as if nothing out of the ordinary had happened.

"Hey, guys." he said.

"This should be good." Colin replied.

"Colin." Nate said, "I sincerely apologize for abruptly leaving you like that."

"Where is it?" Colin asked.

"Where is what?"

"I think you know what I'm talking about." Colin said as he brushed past Nate and headed out the door to his car.

"I had a sudden emergency come up with my dad- I mean, My *dad's* family." Nate said.

Pulling on Nate's back door handle, Colin spoke forcefully, "Please unlock this door!!" As he pulled on the door handle, all he had in mind was regaining possession of the trunk.

"Oh, that thing!" Nate said, "I forgot it was even in there. No wonder you were worried!"

"See, Colin." Carolyn said, "It's all okay. Now let's go enjoy dinner."

Though the trunk was back in his hands, seemingly without any threat toward his quest to open it, Colin was still reluctant to buy the story that Nate had sold so well to his mother. He knew in his heart there was more to it, and he wanted to know what that more was.

During the meal Colin inquired, "So, Nate. What about the family tragedy? That had to have been tough."

"More of a brief emergency; but, you know, it happens every now and then. It's all good now." Nate replied.

"Speaking of tragedy ..." Carolyn said, "I dealt with one first thing this morning. The beautiful vase ... one of three my parents passed down to me ... was on the floor in pieces, completely shattered."

"One of three, you have two more?" asked Nate.

"No." she said, "My two brothers have those."

Carolyn continued, "But, Colin I was about to tell you this earlier. Taped to the inside of it was this key." she said, as she pulled it, along with a piece of the vase, from her pocket.

"I thought it was the strangest thing." she said while looking at it. "Then Colin mentioned finding three key holes inside the trunk when it was opened. Isn't that right, Colin?"

"Uhm." he replied, hating that Nate was a part of the revealing discussion, "Yes."

Nate was soaking in everything that he was hearing and felt as if he was being handed a gold mine's worth of information.

"Three keyholes ... three vases." Carolyn said slowly, "That sounds like something mother would put together."

"Well, Mom. This was a great dinner." Colin said, in hopes of changing the subject.

"Oh, you're welcome, Son."

"Wait." Nate said, "You have one key ... does it fit?"

"We don't have to do all of this right now." Colin said.

"Sure we can ... at least we can try it." Carolyn replied, "Where's that trunk?"

With the trunk top opened and the three keyholes exposed, Carolyn naturally tried placing her key into the top one.

There was no panic when the key did not fit. Instead, she said to Colin, "Read the whole riddle thing over again."

Colin planned on leaving things as they were after the one attempt. Even though he had a good indication of which hole was correct for his mother's key, it was definitely not something that he wanted to pursue in Nate's presence.

At his mother's insistence, Colin read from the paper, "*The search begins where flowers bloom, it …*"

"Flowers bloom … the vase! Okay! I'm just now getting that. How clever!" Carolyn broke in to say. "Keep reading," she continued.

"Hmm … *it ends in a song sung. Keys lined up old too young.*"

Carolyn stopped him again. "That's it. Old to young. My slot is at the bottom." she said as she placed her key into the last hole to find that it was, indeed, a perfect fit.

"Look at us go!!" she said excitedly.

The perfect fit had brightened the outlook for Nate. Knowing that, he excused himself from the table.

"I better get going." he said as he stood up.

"I'll believe it when I see it." Colin murmured. Carolyn nudged him and gave him a look of disappointment. Turning to Nate, she said, "Don't rush off."

"I've got a lot of things to get done, but I sincerely appreciate everything … more than you know."

As Nate drove out on the street, he realized that his dad would be upset that he had not used the key copier, but there had not been an opportune time to do so. He also knew he was leaving with valuable information that he thought would greatly please his father. Nevertheless, there was still a lot of work for him to do to get into the trunk.

Colin retreated to his room after helping clean up the dinner table and dishes. He had a lot of catching up to do for his job. First thing was to explain the updated plans for covering the Harmony Acres venue to his boss at the Castwell Press. The interview delay had sparked a compromise between them that would give Colin more time but would double his work. He would not only be covering the venue but also the first wedding and reception on the property.

The next morning Colin drove Carolyn's van as he headed straight to Harmony Acres. He was early and got there before anyone else arrived. After nearly ten minutes of waiting outside the locked yellow gate, he saw a car driving up behind him. He got out of his car and saw that it was Mary. Her window was rolled down and she was looking at the van.

"Oh, it's you." she said, "I didn't recognize that … thing you're driving."

She got out of her car holding a keyring full of keys. It only took her a few seconds to choose the key that fit the lock on the gate. When the gate was unlocked, she pushed it open and secured it to a post. Colin watched her every move. In spite of the fact that she had been so cool toward him when he made his earlier visit, he held to his hope that this visit would be different.

As she started back to her car, she paused to turn toward Colin and said, "I'm guessing you have something to share with me today."

"Do I ever!" he replied.

Chapter 10

Nate Brewer woke up to find that the most recent intense discussion with his father was still fresh in his mind. Eddie had made it clear to his son that the next steps for them were finding Carolyn's two brothers, Tony and Charlie Webster, and figuring out a way to get their keys to the trunk.

"Do whatever it takes!" his father had emphatically said. Nate could still hear the tone of his father's voice from the night before while he was searching through the Harmony Acres phone number in hopes of reaching Tony's daughter, Mary.

"Harmony Acres, how may I help you?" a voice answered.

"Hi, hey … is Mary Webster available to speak?" he asked.

"Not at the moment, Sir. She's in the middle of her first of many meetings today."

"Do you think she might take a quick minute in between one of them to give me a call? It won't take long at all." Nate said with urgency in his voice.

"Possibly. I'll be happy to take your number and ask her to return your call if she has a

minute to spare."

Nate shared his cell phone number and ended the call. He couldn't help but wonder if he had possibly been beaten to the punch.

Who could she possibly be meeting with this early? It's a wedding venue, for Christ' sake, not the Oval Office.

He did not know it was Colin who had her attention and time at the start of her busy day. She was all ears as she sipped on her coffee while he explained everything that had happened with the trunk and how they should proceed with a plan that would reveal the contents of the trunk.

"I'm not going to lie ... I'm impressed, but even more intrigued." Mary said to him when he finished. She continued, "I just want it to be clear that there's something in 'it', 'it' as in the trunk, for the both of us."

"Well, based on what our grandmother wrote down ..." Colin began to explain while he held the paper back up in front of her. "It seems like there's something in it for all of us ... the whole family."

"Right ... *together again* ... and all that! But, doesn't it just seem right that the ones who found the thing in the first place ... you and me, of course ... should, you know, get a good share of it."

The first words Colin managed to fully grasp from her question were "*you and me.*" In his mind, those three words painted a picture of teamwork between the two of them. That made it easy for him to be okay with accepting Mary's desire to include herself in such a way that their own potential gain should take priority.

When she revealed to him what she saw as the next steps, he knew that she would play a vital part in the process of opening the trunk. "So my dad is supposed to have a vase?"

"Right." Colin said.

"And a key will be taped to the inside of it?"

"Yes, we would certainly hope so."

"I get the key ... it fits ... we have two out of three. What next?" she asked.

"We'll worry about tracking down Uncle Charlie when the time comes. That'll probably be the hardest part." Colin said.

"Well, okay then. Is that everything?" she asked, as she glanced at the clock knowing that she had a full day of work ahead of her.

Colin stood up, "I think so. Oh, wait ... one more thing. I need to get some info on the first couple getting married here. It turns out my editor has me covering the whole wedding."

"Busy guy." Mary said as she looked over some papers, "The groom actually went to school with us. Bruce Williams is his name. Remember him?"

"*Amy...*" Colin said, as he remembered standing beside her a few nights back on the Webster Inn balcony.

"Yeah, he's marrying a girl named Amy Davis. Do you know her?"

"No, not really. Well, kinda sorta. Hardly."

"*Okay.*" Mary quizzically replied, "That's who the couple is, so ..."

"Okay, so yeah ... great. Uhm, so-"

Mary broke in and ended the buffered response, "Come back tomorrow morning. You can talk to them then, and hopefully I'll have the key by then."

Meanwhile ...

Nate Brewer remained in his bedroom until he heard a knock on the door. He opened it to see his father standing there in his pajamas.

"Morning, Son." Eddie said and continued without as much as a pause, "Any progress on your end?"

"Uh ... yeah I think so. I was actually just about to head out."

"I've made some progress myself." Eddie said. "Come here." He signaled him into the other room where Nate saw a trunk placed on the floor.

Startled, Nate began to ask, "What is ..."

"It's a replica ... I had a guy put it together. Your bringing the trunk here the other day turned out to be a good thing after all. I snapped some pictures of it from every angle and sent it to a guy to make. He just dropped this off."

"It's spot on." Nate said while taking a closer look.

Eddie, with his arm around Nate, said, "My Boy, I'm sorry for being hard on you. This is just a really big deal, you know? Roy Webster was the richest man in the county. Whatever he had—or whatever is in that safety storage chest will be a big boost for me ... for us."

Nate asked, "I know, Dad ... I know. So how exactly are we going to swap trunks?"

Eddie replied, "Well, we need someone else ... you know, a distraction. Someone who could also use a little boost."

Nate immediately had an idea of who that could be even though the potential of that person's involvement would be a long stretch. Shortly thereafter, when he lifted the replica to take it to his car outside, he found it to be much lighter in weight than the original one. He soon had it in place inside the car and was on his way. He knew he was going to face a moment that would either make or break the scheme in which he was fully immersed. Nate did his best to retrace the exact route he had taken on the country roads outside of Morriston the day before with Colin. He turned down one that looked familiar and eventually found himself parked behind the lone car in Mr. Jack Anderson's driveway.

"Well, here I go." Nate said to himself as he walked to the front door.

Just after ringing the doorbell, Nate began to get cold feet ... *I can't do this. There's no way!* Until the door slowly opened.

With a newspaper in his hand, Mr. Anderson asked, "Morning! May I help you, Sir?"

"Hey there, Mr. Anderson. It's Nate-"

"Wait a second ... let me finish it." Mr. Anderson chimed in, "Brewer?"

"Oh, wow. That's it." said Nate.

"Nate Brewer!" Mr. Anderson exclaimed, "Class of ... just kidding, I'm not *that* good. Come on in ... what can I do for you?"

"I believe Colin Webster was here yesterday."

"That's right." Mr. Anderson replied, "Wasn't that you who left him here?"

"Guilty."

"Colin said something about his family's trunk being in your car. He was worried sick about that thing. Did he get it back?"

"Oh, yes. He did." Nate replied. "That was actually what I came here to talk about. I'm planning on a little surprise for Colin. I know how much he admires you, and I am just wondering if you want to play a part in it."

"Sure, I'd be happy to."

"The first step is for him to come here. When he gets here, you'll let me know. He'll most definitely have the trunk ... which I'll take ... and then ..."

"Hold on one second." Mr. Anderson said, "I see where this is going."

"You do?"

"You want the trunk, right?"

"Well, I-"

Mr. Anderson broke in again, "I mean, it's no secret who once owned that trunk and what could possibly be in that thing. Colin said that whatever it is would bring the family together, but you and I both know what that could really mean."

Nate, feeling exposed, could only give a defeated nod as he began to regret the approach he had taken that appeared to put a bind on the entire plan.

Wanting a clear response, Mr. Anderson continued, "So I'll ask again. You want the trunk, right? Yes, or no?"

Nate could only think of his father's expectation as he gave an answer that was not truly his own. Unconvincingly, he replied, "Yes."

Mr. Anderson, a natural teacher with a newly wide open schedule, looked at the broken man in front of him. He knew immediately that he had found his next assignment, and he needed to fill it.

"So tell me, Nate." he replied, "How are we going to get it?"

"You want in?" asked Nate.

"Yes, I do. I think Colin is due for a *good* surprise."

The surprises began early the next morning for Colin. After arriving at the venue even earlier than the day before, he sat in the vehicle and waited for Mary to arrive yet again. When she drove up, she did not immediately get out of her car to unlock the gate.

Colin heard his phone ding and looked to see that she had sent him a text message. Opening it, he read her text message that simply said, "Come here."

When he got to her car, Mary, rolled down her window and, said, "I'm doing my best to preserve these nice shoes that I'm wearing today. Walking in these woods wouldn't help that." she continued, "Here, take this."

Colin took the key which Mary handed to him and headed to the entrance gate while she continued to dig through her tote bag looking for her key ring. When she looked up holding the key ring in her hand, she saw that Colin was struggling to try to fit the key she had given him into the gate lock. He looked back toward Mary and saw her holding a ring full of keys.

With her thumb and index finger on the proper one for the gate, Colin realized that the first key Mary had given him didn't fit the gate lock because it must be …. "Is this *the one*?" he asked her. Minutes later, they were in her office with the trunk on her desk; and the key that she handed him fit perfectly into the top key hole on the trunk. The answer was clear … it was.

Their moment of excitement quickly led Colin and Mary to discussing their difficult next steps to get the proper key for the middle slot. Based on the trend they had both noticed, if anyone had the key, it would most likely be the middle child in the Webster family. Getting in touch with their uncle, Charlie Webster, was the final obstacle and their only hope. He was the one who had always been considered the oddball of the family. He had always liked to do things his own way, even when the family was relatively well connected. He had, in fact, played a big role in the family diverging onto separate paths.

The one piece of information about him that Colin and Mary did have was valuable enough to serve as their launching pad.

"The Harbor Pointe beach house." Mary said to Colin.

Thinking about the piece of family property that had been put in Charlie's name, Colin asked, "Do you think he'd still be there?"

"Well, I asked my dad about that yesterday when I went to look for his key. He said the odds of him still living there comfortably after all this time were slim, but he really has no clue."

"Slim is better than none, I guess." Colin said.

"I'll try to do some research." Mary said, "Do you remember the street it was on?"

"How could I forget? Ocean Way." Colin replied, "But do you want me to do all of that? As a journalist, I'm used to it."

"I'll handle it." Mary told him, "Besides, you need time to do what brought you here in the first place … your actual job, remember?"

"Oh, yes, I guess you're right."

"Bruce and Amy are on their way here now. You can go out and interview them while I take your place as the distracted one."

Colin stood outside as he waited for the couple to arrive. Making sure to rid himself of any distractions, he ignored the vibrating phone in his pocket. Focusing became much easier when he saw the car that was driving in his direction. He recognized it right way as the car he and Nate had passed along the wooded path. Seeing Amy alone in the vehicle, Colin became all the more focused.

Just as she did the last time she saw Colin, Amy tried to hide her true emotions that the coincidental encounter with him provoked. She took her time getting out of the car, waiting for him to speak. It wasn't until she was near him that he did.

"Ma'am- uh … Ms. Davis." Colin said.

Amy looked up to face him and removed her sunglasses.

"Well, look who is here." she said. With a hand up, Amy continued, "Don't worry, I'm not smoking."

"Ha, right." Colin replied, "I'm not here to tell you what to do, I just need to ask some questions before you meet with Mary."

"Oh, that may be even worse."

"I'm a journalist with the Castwell Press and I'm doing a story on this venue. I am also assigned to cover the first wedding … that being your wedding."

"How flattering." Amy said with an air of disinterest.

"Is your fiancé on the way here or …?" Colin asked.

"No, I just put him in charge of the reception music. I think I'd be smoking a lot more if he did much else."

"Gotcha! Well, shall we begin?" asked Colin.

"Sure." Amy replied as she took the first steps. Their walk eventually led them to a bench closer to the lake.

By the time they were seated on the bench, the conversation had taken a more personal turn.

"I get it now." Amy said, after answering many questions that Colin had asked about the upcoming wedding, "You're so good at asking questions that you don't even know how to answer them."

"Meaning?"

"Meaning that you're pretty good at covering something of which you want no part … Mr. Noncommittal."

"Oh." Colin said as he realized what Amy was implying. "Well … it just … it changes people. You know! They drop everything that makes them who they really are and alter themselves in an attempt to blend perfectly with another person."

"That's what it's all about, right?" Amy asked, seeing herself in his example.

"If it is, I don't want any part of it."

"Wow, someone must have *really* hurt you." Amy said, reminding him of what had been left unanswered from their last encounter. "I don't know who, but they sure did leave a scar. Poor thing."

Colin felt like Amy was picking at a scab. To avoid any further bleeding, he felt he should end the conversation. "I think I have enough for today, we can finish later. I need to get going."

As she watched him walk away, Amy remained seated on the bench and reexamined the perspective that he had shared with her. As she did, she began to feel less confident in her own.

Moments later, Colin entered Mary's office where he encountered an aura that anyone else would have seen as the epitome of a major breakthrough. Colin, however, was coming face to face with the answer to Amy's question.

"Jackpot." Mary said as she held up a flyer for him to see with the bold letters that read *Estate Sale.* "Uncle Charlie's money problems have worked out in our favor, I guess." she continued.

Colin soberly grabbed the flyer that she had printed out, and, while reading the details about the Harbor Pointe beach house estate sale set for the next day, he told Mary, "Half of the *happy* couple is out there ready to meet with you."

"Okay, but isn't this big?" she asked with enthusiasm.

"Yeah. No, it really is."

"I mean, you'd think a valuable vase would be one of the items for sale, right?"

"Yeah, maybe so. You never know." Colin replied, "Then the dreaded search would be over." while the thought of shifting back to normalcy sparked a hope that it would last a little longer.

After agreeing to meet at the venue first thing the next morning, Colin left the office and walked back to his mother's van ... a vehicle that he was sick of driving. Before leaving, he checked his cellphone and saw the ignored call had been from Mr. Jack Anderson, who had also left a voicemail.

Colin played it to hear, "Hey there, Colin. Jack Anderson here. Give me a call back when you get the chance."

When Colin did, he noticed that Mr. Anderson was very quick to answer.

"Hey, Colin!"

"How's it going, sir?"

"Well, it's-it's going ... would you mind stopping by here at some point today?" Mr. Anderson asked.

"Oh, okay. Is everything alright?"

"Of course, I just needed a hand with something."

When the quick call ended, Mr. Anderson began another one as he scrambled to figure out what exactly he would need help with.

"Nate." he said over the phone, "He's on his way ... you can head over but keep your distance."

Colin drove straight to Mr. Anderson's house from the Harmony Acres venue and was welcomed inside by his former teacher who appeared very happy to see him.

"I need this couch pushed over to get a better view of the television. I would do it myself, but my doctor doesn't want an old guy straining his back."

"That's no problem." Colin said as he got in position to move the couch.

After barely pushing the couch to a slightly different angle, Mr. Anderson stopped him and stood behind it, and looked at the television.

"Yep." he told Colin, "That's the spot ... perfect."

"Oh. Well, alright then. Is that all?"

"I think so, but since you took the time to come here, I'd hate for you to turn around and leave so soon."

"It's no problem at all." Colin replied.

"So how are things going with your 'family together again' project?"

"They're going ... almost too well."

Mr. Anderson knew what he meant and had begun to feel the same way himself as every step in the plan was working in his favor. At the same time that Colin shared every update about the trunk with his former teacher, Nate slowly drove away from his parked spot on the other side of the street and eased in the direction of Mr. Anderson's driveway. Before reaching it, he stopped and parked alongside the street. Toting the replica trunk, Nate left his car and hurried over to the van. He could only hope that Mr. Anderson would keep Colin distracted long enough for him to exchange the replica and the original trunk.

Nate sat the replica down and reached in his pocket to pull out a small slip of paper with a four-digit code that would unlock the van door.

After pressing *6483* on the door's number keypad, the van was unlocked, the original trunk was moved out, and the replica was placed in its spot.

Nate was able to appreciate the nearly identical similarities between the two trunks with only minor differences that would never be noticed without them being side by side. The exchange was possible thanks to a small task that Carolyn had presented him with one night — retrieving some papers inside her van. He realized then that helping out at the Webster Inn had officially paid dividends. Also quickly understood was the heaviness of the original trunk that was in stark contrast to the replica that he had easily carried over from his car that suddenly seemed so far away. Nate's wavering strength produced the ultimate struggle. By the time he reached his parked car in front of the next yard over, he turned to see the track that he had left behind after being forced to drag the trunk along the grass.

Mr. Anderson nervously watched the entire episode unfold from inside the house, while, at the same time, staying engaged in conversation with Colin. He was able to loosen up only after seeing that Nate was in the clear, finally driving away. It was not long before Colin did the same thing once Mr. Anderson wrapped up their conversation and was very appreciative to him for stopping by to help in more ways than he knew.

After Mr. Anderson stood on his front porch to wave as Colin backed out of the driveway, he was quick to get Nate back on the phone.

"Nate." he said, "We have a big morning tomorrow. Be here first thing."

Chapter 11

Colin went back home and spent the rest of his day keeping himself busy with the many jobs on his long to-do list. On the landscaping end, a tall stack of stones was to be placed along the flower beds, causing a lot of heavy lifting, and, ultimately, a back that he knew would be sore. That job made everything else on the list seem much lighter, including the trunk that he removed from his mother's van and placed back in his car after his time under the hood was completed. When Colin made his way back inside to clean up for dinner, he felt very accomplished. He felt sure the car would be okay for the summer and he could now avoid a professional mechanic.

To close out the long day, Colin found himself where he spent most of his nights. Seated at his desk looking at his laptop screen, he edited the list of questions that he had yet to ask cousin Mary about her business, even adding a few more that had been accumulating in his mind over the years. The next morning, Colin was at the place where he had spent the past several mornings. He was more than happy to continually return to Harmony Acres as the commercialization that had been painted over the properties' natural colors seemed to rub off during each visit.

Colin found Mary in her car. She appeared to be ready to get a move on. He put his work bag around his shoulder, grabbed the trunk without even thinking about its weight, and opened Mary's back door to put it in.

"Be careful with that thing." she told him, "The car is new."

"Don't worry." Colin replied, having already picked up on that fact after taking one look at the vehicle's luxurious exterior.

Seated on the passenger side, Colin breathed in the fresh smell of the interior, and said, "Wow, business must be going well for you."

It would be the last words that Colin could bring himself to say for most of the car ride. The loud music playing on the radio filled the void caused by their lack of words. He pulled out the list of questions that were a top priority for his story and slowly scanned it. He imagined how it would have been asking them in the past when conversation was so effortless between the two of them. His mind was totally focused on the paper until he looked up to see that they were approaching the Harbor Pointe bridge.

"Well, here we are." Colin said as Harbor Pointe Island appeared before him for the first time in years.

Both of Mary's hands felt sweaty as they gripped the steering wheel. She was internally recapping her own history on the island with growing angst. She took a deep breath, and, thought to herself, "Yep ... here it is."

After a long upward slope, Mary's car had reached the bridge's highest point where the entire Harbor Pointe island was visible. The enthusiasm between the two cousins was on the opposite ends of the spectrum. The memories in each of their minds were coming from very different perspectives.

Once they had crossed the bridge and were in Harbor Pointe, Colin broke the silence between them. "You know ... I'm feeling pretty good about this!"

Mary remained silent and sat stiffly as she could only think of her sinking level of confidence. The drive down the slope had reminded her of her inner feeling which continued to plummet all the way to their destination. When she reached 156 Ocean Way, she spoke up, "What's going on here? This is the right place, isn't it?"

"Looks different." Colin said as he viewed the Webster family's former vacation spot.

Mary observed the obvious, "That might be because there's a driveway full of tables that those people are looking at."

After struggling to find a place to park along the crowed street full of cars, Colin and Mary walked up the side of the street and onto the driveway. They both were assuming that all the cars were overflow parking from the nearby public beach access. However, as they neared the house, they saw the line of people waiting to get inside. They both immediately realized what was happening.

"Are estate sales always this big of a deal around here?" Colin asked a man waiting near the back of the line.

"Not usually, but this is completely different." the man said.

"How so?" asked Colin.

"Have you heard of the Webster family?"

Hearing that, Colin turned to Mary. The two of them simultaneously made their way through the line that wrapped around two flights of wooden stairs outside. Those steps led to an open door on the second floor that entered into the spacious upstairs living room area where more tables were spread around with various items filling each one.

Ahead of them was a woman who looked like she was in charge of the large operation. As they approached her, Mary sensed that she was her kind of person. "Let me do the talking," she whispered to Colin.

She began, "Hi there, ma'am-"

"If you have any questions ask the gentleman over there holding the clipboard." the lady was quick to say.

Oh, God love her. Mary thought to herself before replying, "Actually ... I have more of a statement to make; but before I do, I wanted to introduce myself. I am Mary *Webster* ... and this is my cousin, Colin *Webster*."

She had successfully gained the attention of the woman, but with a different approach than Colin would have taken. To not to roll his eyes at Mary's heavy emphasis on their last name required all the stamina that he had.

The lady began to ask, "As in-"

"Yes ... Come to think about it, I ... we ... have a question." Mary said as she pulled Colin in closer in order to include him.

Then Mary nudged him and said, "Take it away, Colin." He responded, "Oh, I'm allowed to speak now? Okay. Well, there's a specific item we were wondering about. It's a vase ... a vase that is really important to our family and ..."

The lady interrupted, "Does it have a particular look or?"

"No, not really, but …"

Mary, growing impatient, broke in, "Ultimately, there's a key that we need."

"So am I looking for a key or a vase?" the lady questioned.

"Both." Mary said, "The key would be inside the vase."

Can you give me an idea of what either one would specifically look like?" the lady asked.

"Actually, we can! Right?" Mary asked Colin, "Don't we have the trunk with two keys already in it?"

Colin, understood that was her way of telling him to go get them and held out his hand for Mary's car keys. He walked down the stairs and through the line of people catching the eyes from most of those waiting to get inside after they saw him pass by a second time.

At last, Colin thought when he reached the car that was several blocks from the house.

He unlocked the car doors. The trunk was resting on the floor mat between the front passenger seat and the one behind it. Needing more space to get it opened, Colin lifted it up with ease. He immediately knew something was off. He pulled the trunk up on the backseat and quickly flipped up the two knobs. Before trying to open it, he prepared himself for the worst case scenario. That strategy did very little to soften the blow of what he saw when he opened the trunk … actually it was what he did not see that hit him the hardest.

Not only were the two keys missing, the holes they were supposed to be inserted into were nowhere to be found on the trunk's black wooden cover.

Inside the house where Mary waited for Colin, the news was no better. It did however, come with a slight upside. After checking the long list of items available, the lady in charge informed Mary that there was not even one vase or key available.

"So you're telling me that, out of all this stuff, there's nothing?" Mary asked.

"No." the lady said. "If you were looking for elaborate pieces of art or random animal statues that money was blown on, you'd be in luck."

"Well, okay then. I guess I'll go save my cousin from taking another trip back up here."

Before Mary walked away, the lady said, "Wait." She reached in her pocket and pulled out a business card. Handing it to Mary, she said, "This is the firm that represents your ...?"

"Uncle." Mary said.

"Yes, your uncle. If you wanted to know more about his situation or what you're looking for, they could possibly help. It'd be worth a try."

"It's better than nothing." Mary said as she took the business card and briefly glanced at the last names. "James, Baxter & Hunt" was printed in bold letters across the top of it.

Mary met Colin halfway between the house and where the car was parked. She could tell immediately that something was wrong by his despondent look. Her suspicion was confirmed without the use of words as she held out her arms with a look of question on her face. Colin responded by giving a thumbs down and pointing in the direction of the car.

"It's gone, Mary. The trunk, our chances of opening it, this whole experiment. It's all over ... back to reality."

Inside, once the car had been started and their seat belts buckled, Mary finally asked, "What on earth happened?"

Colin explained how he had easily lifted the trunk to the car seat and suspicioned that something was wrong ... and the condition in which he had found the trunk.

"What? How?" was all Mary knew to say as she pulled out of the space where she had parked and began to drive away. Seeing Colin's frustration and feeling her own confusion, she decided to put off asking anything else at the moment.

She headed back down the street in the direction from which they had come. As they passed the Webster house she spoke, "You know, that lady gave me the information on Uncle Charlie's attorneys and ..."

"That's great and all, but there's really no use for that." Colin replied.

The only thing that had any meaningful use for him at that moment was the sign they passed shortly after leaving the island and crossing the Harbor Pointe bridge. In the same font style from decades before, the big letters on the sign read, "Del's Drive In."

With lunchtime approaching, Colin spoke up, "You hungry?"

"I really should go ahead and get back." Mary replied.

"Oh, come on." Colin said. "For old time's sake. Just think … when will we ever be back here to do this? Probably never."

Mary gave in just in time to make the turn into the parking lot where there were a good number of cars with people waiting for their food. She did so without realizing that it would create the perfect stretch of time for Colin to start an exchange of personal dialogue between the two of them. Little did he expect Mary's vulnerability would be so easy to expose.

Once Mary had parked near the back of the lot behind the other cars, Colin spoke over the sound of music coming from the car radio and said, "I bet you're relieved."

"There's nothing about this wait that's relieving." Mary replied.

"No." Colin replied as he turned the radio volume all the way down and continued, "The fact that you can go back to work and forget about this whole ordeal."

"Oh. Well, I mean, I guess so. I don't know, it's still work."

"Yeah but you're so in your element. Doing your thing at a place like the lake … it can't get much better than that."

"It's really not that easy … you don't know the half of it." Mary said as she reached over to turn the volume back up. Colin put his hand on hers to stop her.

"Of course I don't." he said, with his own vulnerability growing, "That's what happens when you're … you're just shut off … you don't know things anymore."

"You wouldn't want to know." Mary responded as she looked directly into his eyes.

"I can take it! I mean … at one point I was the first one to know everything!"

"Okay, great! Now you can be the *only* one to know how sad I am … how miserable my job can be … how much of a drag it is to just get out of bed to go make sure the happiest day of someone else's life is perfect. All the while having to constantly forget about mine!"

Mary caught her breath as Colin asked, "So why are you still doing it?"

"Because … it's all I have." Mary replied, "I know I'd be in an even worse place without it. Doing this suddenly became the distraction that I needed, you know?"

"Trust me, I do." Colin said as he looked ahead, It's-"

Knock, knock

They both turned to see the young waitress outside Mary's window. When she rolled it down, the girl asked, "Are you guys ready to order?"

This ended Colin's chance to share what was on his heart before it could begin.

****

It was while they were giving their orders that Mr. Anderson and Nate Brewer passed by the drive-in on the main road as they finally neared Harbor Pointe. Mr. Anderson was not lying when he told Nate that they would have a busy morning as he took full advantage of having a chauffeur. After using the trip towards the Harbor Pointe area as one extended errand that he had been putting off, Mr. Anderson pulled out his Day-Timer and tested his acting ability.

"Oh, no." he said as he flipped through the pages.

"What is it?" asked Nate as he continued to concentrate on the road ahead of him.

"I've messed up and gotten ahead of myself … we didn't need to come down this way today."

Nate, unaware of the other agenda Mr. Anderson had in mind, tried to present an understanding reaction to the older gentleman's mix-up. He replied, "Well, it wasn't a complete waste of a trip, I guess." He was appreciative of any time away from his father's oversight.

Seeing the potential in what could come out of a nice meal, Mr. Anderson suggested, "How about let's turn around and stop for lunch on the way back. It's on me."

****

Back at Del's Drive-In, Colin and Mary finished up their meals. The good tasting food, however, was no fix for the struggles that were weighing on each of them. On the drive back to Morriston, Colin, after hearing Mary's spill on the true nature of her job, knew better than to mention anything about it or anything else.

****

Their drive could not have differed more from what was going on in Mr. Anderson's car. He and Nate Brewer continued their banter that had begun at the restaurant table. It continued until they suddenly found themselves back at Mr. Anderson's house. Their trip seemed to have flown by. Jack Anderson learned that even though he had made a career at teaching information to people, he was even better at pulling it out. Like he had with Colin, it was done in such a casual way that it disguised his purposeful efforts entirely. The light-hearted exchange of heavy, revealing subjects made sharing such things much easier for Nate.

"I really needed this." he told Mr. Anderson, "For a while there I had forgotten about the reason we were out in the first place."

Jack Anderson had never forgotten; and he made sure to bring it up when he replied, "I'll get back up with you tomorrow about the correct date for Harbor Pointe. We're going to get that trunk opened, don't you worry."

When he entered his home, he headed straight toward a thick book that he kept near the landline telephone. The book was titled "Student Info." Mr. Anderson opened it and flipped past the A and B letters then stopped at C. He found the name "Charlie Webster" and took a look at the number beside one of the first students that he had ever taught. He dialed the number into his cellphone.

"Charlie! It's Jack here … when are you working again? I was thinking about heading over there. It's been too long." he said in hopes of meeting directly with the source.

****

When it came to a source, Colin Webster was left scrambling for one on which his article about Harmony Acres could focus. However, when he arrived back there with Mary, he found his last hope waiting for them.

"Have you been here long?" Mary asked the soon-to-be bride, Amy Davis.

Amy replied, "Not really, no."

As the two of them headed for the office to make final plans for Amy's upcoming wedding, Colin spoke up, "Hey, Amy."

She turned to face him as he continued, "I'd like to finish that interview once your meeting is done. Is that okay?"

Amy remained straight faced as she nodded and softly replied, "Yes ... sure we can do that."

Colin nodded and pointed over to the same lakeside bench where the first part of the interview had taken place. "I'll meet you over there." he said as he headed in that direction. Arriving at the bench, he sat down in hopes of clearing his head before continuing the interview.

He had yet to begin when, from behind him, he heard Amy's voice, "Now you know how it feels to sit there alone."

"That was fast." Colin turned to say.

"Yeah. Actually all the planning is complete. I just had to take care of the paying part."

No wonder Mary was in a hurry to get back ... He thought to himself before replying, "That doesn't sound like as much fun as the planning."

"Honestly, none of it has been fun." she said. "This whole process has just been overwhelming, especially doing most of it by myself."

"Well, if you don't mind." Colin said, "The real fun of answering some questions can begin."

"If *you* don't mind," Amy said, "I'd rather do that somewhere else."

"Oh, well okay. We can walk around or-"

"How about a drive?" Amy asked.

"Whatever works best for you." Colin replied as he stood up from the bench.

They approached the parked cars in front of the office, and Colin instinctively began walking towards his own. Hesitantly, Amy asked, "Are you sure that thing will start?"

"Honestly ... no."

"I'd like to feel some control." Amy said, "I'll just drive mine; come on."

"Control, huh?" asked Colin as he sat in yet another passenger seat.

"Believe it or not, it seems like driving a car is about all the control I have at this point."

"Aren't you the one that's planning the wedding?"

"I can only think of it as planning for the start of a lifelong seat in the background."

Colin, hoping to shift away from the melancholy mood, asked, "So, you and Bruce. How did you two meet and come together?"

"Well it was-" Amy began, "Actually, you know what? I really don't want to talk about this kind of stuff … him or the wedding."

"So why do you think I'm here?" Colin asked.

"Well, you can talk about yourself." Amy suggested as she neared the highway exit.

"No, that's okay. You're not going to drive me to my death, are you?"

"If I take this exit and drive straight, where would we end up?"

"Uhm, Harbor Pointe beach, I guess. But I really should head back and-"

"Beach?!" Amy exclaimed, "That's the safest way to use my extreme spontaneity right now."

Realizing that there were worse places he could be, Colin was willing to go to any of them if it meant making progress on the article that held much importance for his job. With that, Colin found himself sitting back to take another trip to Harbor Pointe for the second time in one day.

****

That evening in her office back at the Harmony Acres venue, Mary Webster sat alone with the James, Baxter & Hunt law firm business card she had been given on the desk in front of her. It was the first name among the three, James, that had her suddenly hesitant to type the firm's web address listed on the card into her computer.

Ugh, this is ridiculous. What am I doing? She asked herself before taking hold of the computer mouse and clicking into the search bar to begin typing. Mary hit the enter key. The lake property's spotty wi-fi caused extra loading time, but soon the firm's website appeared on the screen. She clicked on the "About Us" page. Though three images of the firm's partners appeared, Mary's eyes were fixed on only one of them. The name under the photo was "Lee James." He was the man who was responsible for many of her memories at Harbor Pointe. However, the best of those memories had been overtaken by a single event that had kept a big part of her heart closed ever since.

With the same courage that she used earlier that day to enter back onto the island to which she had once vowed never to return, Mary dialed in the phone number under his name. She began the call without really believing that Lee would still be working that late into the evening. She did not really anticipate the possibility of him answering … until he did.

Chapter 12

"Lee James here, how may I help you?"

"Oh-uh. Yeah, Hi."

"Hello?"

"Hey, Lee. You're not going to believe this. It's Mary Webster."

"Mary!" Lee cheerfully said, "It's so good to hear your voice! How are you?"

"Oh … I-I'm doing good. You?"

"I can't complain. Who knew a good surprise could come from staying late at the office? What are you up to these days?"

"Wow, where to begin. Well, I-"

"Wait." Lee said, "I'd hate to catch up over the phone. Would you like to get together for a coffee or something? There's some things that, for years, I have regretted not saying to you. It would only be right to do it face to face."

"You can just apologize to me over the phone … it's fine."

"No, it's more than that … really."

"Oh, I don't know. The reason I called was to …"

"Please, Mary. For old time's sake."

Giving into those four words for the second time that day, Mary replied, "Alright … alright. I guess that'd be okay."

****

Colin was also experiencing his own short form of *de ja vu* at the same moment. The sun had officially set, and he looked ahead to see the lights shining on Harbor Point Island at the bridge's highest point.

"What a sight!" Amy said, seeing that same view for the first time.

Per her request, everything discussed during the lengthy car ride to the beach was off the record. Though Colin initially had every reason to wonder what his purpose was on the surprise trip, it did not take him long to find out how valuable a badly needed listening ear was to Amy.

Even while stopped at a red light, Amy fidgeted — the impulsive energy had only grown since their departure from Harmony Acres. She looked ahead and saw something that caught her attention. It was a large sign that stood front and center while glowing brightly in the night. It read, "Harbor Circle: Where Memories Are Made."

"I don't know about you, but I want to go there." she said. "Is it true? Are memories made at the Harbor Circle?"

"Honestly, I've never been there." Colin said of the popular public beach access spot. "My family and I would always go to the Harbor Pointe Beach Club that's farther down the street."

"Oh, excuse me. How fancy!" Amy playfully said, "That'll change tonight. A memory will be made even if it's the last thing I do!"

As she quickly swerved over to the next lane that went straight ahead to the circle, Colin wondered if Amy's attempt to get there would actually be the last thing he did. When they arrived at the sparsely populated beach area, it seemed to Colin that the people there could not possibly be up to any good. It was Amy who dragged him along while not noticing anyone or anything but the roaring sound of the ocean that was ahead of them.

After running at a pace that was close to a sprint, she removed her shoes and tossed them aside, and yelled, "Come on!" to Colin.

Many steps behind, he did his best to keep up. At the same time, he was wondering if he should go back to retrieve the items that Amy had left behind in the unlocked car. Colin persevered while thinking of the worst scenarios that could happen behind him and beginning to think of new ones that could lie ahead. He wondered if Amy would ever slow down before being swept away by the sea. Seeing that she finally did, Colin stopped just short of where she stood in the ankle-deep water.

Amy gazed out at the dark ocean that was lit only by the moon above and caught her breath while doing so. She then faced Colin and, with a look of pure sincerity, said, "Hey, Colin?"

"Yeah?"

"What kind of moron wears shoes on a beach?" She was looking down at his shoes which he had not taken off.

"Oh, please." he replied as she walked toward him and took a seat on the sand.

"I mean, I may not go to the beach often, but I think it's a valid question." she continued.

"Yeah, yeah." Colin responded as he sat down on the sand. He made sure to leave a comfortable distance between them before continuing, "I think I have a valid question …"

Amy looked over to him after he paused for a beat.

"Are you really going to marry him?"

Colin faced the ocean before asking the blunt question in order to avoid any direct eye contact with Amy. She was also looking out over the ocean. Hearing nothing in response, from the corner of his left eye, he saw her begin to lean back. Colin finally turned his head to see her. Her eyes were facing upwards in the direction of the few stars that were in the sky, while her elbows were planted in the sand.

"You know, Colin … I only want to focus on what's right in front of me."

At that point, their faces turned and they stared intently into each other's eyes. Amy continued, "Right here, right now."

The distance Colin had intentionally left between them prevented any physical contact. Amy lightened the mood and said, "Well, this was fun!" as she got up and brushed the sand off her arms.

Colin waited a moment to make sure his tongue was not tied and replied, "Yeah-yeah, it was. I'm glad you dragged me out here, really."

As they made their exit from the beach and headed toward her car, Colin offered, "I can drive back if you want."

"Yeah, that'd be fine … but are you sure you know how to drive a functioning vehicle?"

Colin was very sure that he did, but once behind the wheel he quickly learned that the car could practically drive itself. He also had a better sense of how it felt to have a question left unanswered. It sparked a desire to randomly revisit one that she had brought up on multiple occasions.

"Mary!" he said aloud in the car that was much quieter on the drive away from the beach. "My cousin, Mary. Your wedding planner, Mary Webster."

"Huh?"

"You asked who hurt me ... it was her."

"I see."

"It was this guy ... from Harbor Pointe actually. He just had such a stronghold on her and it changed everything, you know? He had this effect on everything that she did. I've seen a lot of distorted images of love in my life, that being one of them. I guess it hurt me and my approach to love. So there ... That's my answer."

****

That same guy was the reason for Mary's drive all the way back to Harbor Pointe the next day. The anxious feeling that had come over her the day before on the bridge resurfaced as soon as she left home for her evening with Lee. Her mood changed only when she arrived at his house and saw an elegant vase filled with flowers through his large front window. The vase reminded Mary of her sole purpose for ever coming back to the island, the reason she had acquired the law firm's business card. The card had made the phone call with Lee possible. The call with Lee had led to her arrival at his house less than twenty-four hours later.

Mary's mind shifted when she decided to connect this meeting to that purpose. Viewing it in a more business-like manner calmed her nerves as she walked up the front steps to Lee's opulent home. That viewpoint, however, faded slightly when Lee James opened the door with a smile that suddenly reminded Mary of how she had once fallen in love with him.

"Mary." he said in his low, but comfortably soft voice. "It's so good to see you."

Mary's hand brushed through her hair as she faced him and replied, "Yes, likewise. It's been quite a while."

"Where has the time gone?" he asked her.

"It really does fly by." Mary replied, looking up and past Lee to spot another flower-filled vase in a different window behind him. Having trouble taking her eyes off of it, she said, "I'm sorry, but that vase is just so beautiful. Someone has really done a good job decorating around here. As a wedding planner, I have high standards … and I am impressed."

"Oh, really? Thanks! My uncle was just here earlier. He said it looked like a funeral home, so I'm glad you think that."

Mary was quickly reminded of why she was there as a voice inside her head screamed, *Uncle!* It led to her to say, "I actually forgot to mention *my* Uncle, Charlie Webster, over the phone last night. I think your firm represents him."

"That's right! We sure do. I can't believe I didn't put two and two together to make that connection."

"Do you know what he's up to?" she asked.

"Well, he's had a tough time financially since his divorce. As a bankruptcy lawyer, he keeps me busy. The good news is that he's just recently started working as a waiter at the beach country club. I've seen him there the past few times that I have been."

"Interesting." she replied before Lee continued. "Speaking of the beach club, I was wondering if you wanted to have an early dinner there."

Thoughts about summers spent at the club were interrupted by the possibility of seeing Uncle Charlie there. It was that fact that prompted Mary's enthusiastic response of, "That'd be great!"

As they passed the other extravagant homes on their way out of the neighborhood, Mary observed, "What a nice place to live."

"I love it." Lee replied, "The people living around here are even nicer than their houses."

"So it's just you living in yours?" Mary asked, knowing it was of a similar size as the other large ones.

Giving Mary no other choice but to be impressed, Lee replied, "For now, yes." in a smooth but humble manner that was seamed together perfectly.

Upon their arrival, Mary was equally, if not more so, amazed at the vast improvements that had been made to the clubhouse since her last time there.

Once Lee drove under the front portico and handed his car keys to the valet, they entered the luxurious clubhouse and savored the aroma of fresh seafood.

Almost immediately after they walked inside, Lee said to Mary, "I've reserved a table in the upstairs room." He pointed to the staircase, "You go ahead ... I'll be right up."

Mary ascended the stairs and went into the lone dining room on the second floor. The room was filled with empty tables. Seeing nobody else and thinking there must have been a mix-up, Mary turned to walk back down the stairs before seeing a waiter making his way up.

"Good evening, ma'am." he said, "Is everything okay?"

"I'm a guest of Lee James. He reserved a table up here but there isn't anyone else ... so-"

"Oh, Mr. James reserved the entire room." said the waiter, "I'll be taking care of you guys tonight."

"Wow. Okay then, great." she replied. She knew then that the club dinner was no spur-of-the-moment plan for Lee.

Downstairs, just as Lee left the restroom to join Mary, he was approached by another member.

"Well, I declare. Another one?" the man asked Lee.

Lee smirked and asked, "What do you mean?"

"Don't think I didn't notice your plus one."

"This one's different. There's history." Lee replied.

"I don't know how you do it." the man said while shaking his head.

"What can I say ... I'm experienced." said Lee, as he began making his way up the stairs.

When he entered his reserved room, he found Mary staring at the view of the dunes and the ocean from the large window where they were to have dinner.

"Never gets old." he said to her before repeating himself and referring to something else entirely, "It *never* does get old." He took his seat across from her.

It was there that they watched the sunlight dim and eventually set over the ocean while enjoying the three-course meal that was brought up to them. Well after the last bite of dessert was finished, they reminisced about the times they once shared and recapped the time they had lost as well. It was with full stomachs and equally full hearts that they eventually got up from their seats to leave.

Lee asked Mary, "Do you want to meet outside? I need to find our waiter and take care of his tip."

"That's fine."

Watching him hurry down the stairs, Mary remembered that she had failed to inquire of anyone at the club about Uncle Charlie. Before exiting the clubhouse, Mary approached a gentleman in a waiter's uniform who was cleaning up the buffet table.

"Excuse me, Sir." she said.

"Yes? I mean … how may I help you? I'm sorry … it's late." said the young man.

"No worries, I just had a quick question. Would you happen to know Charlie Webster? I believe he works here."

"Uhm. *Charlie Webster?*" he thought aloud, before asking his co-worker who was passing by, "Hey, is there a Charlie Webster that works here?"

"Yeah." the co-worker replied, "You know, he's the older guy that just started recently."

"Oh yeah!" the young man replied.

Mary broke in and asked, "Is he working tonight?"

"No, ma'am. I don't think so. He should be here tomorrow, though."

"Yeah." the co-worker said, "I saw his name on the schedule."

"Perfect, thanks." Mary said, "That's all I needed to know."

With that new piece of information, Mary pulled out her phone to text a message sharing the news with Colin.

From the restroom door that was ajar and with his fellow club member's observation in mind, Lee James watched and waited for Mary to leave the clubhouse. When she finally did, the coast was cleared for him to do the same thing. Unlike their entrance, Lee put more thought into keeping an unnoticeable distance from Mary while he waited for the valet to return his car to the front portico. His actions were masterfully orchestrated, showing the "experience" that he had mentioned earlier. Mary had no indication whatsoever that anything out of the ordinary was happening. When their time together came to an end that evening, Mary had been given every right to believe that she would be seeing more of Lee James in the near future.

For Colin, the trunk's disappearance had given him less of a right to have any belief. His doubts about Mary's plan to see Uncle Charlie were expressed briefly over the phone and directly to her the next morning when she showed up to pick him up for yet another trip to Harbor Pointe.

After sluggishly approaching her car, Colin got in and asked, "Why exactly are we doing this?" knowing that the trunk was long gone and thinking of the full Saturday he could spend catching up on work.

"I had a thought." Mary said. "We might not need whatever was in that trunk to bring the family together."

"I didn't think you cared about that."

"Well, that *was* true. Family aside, I kind of experienced that whole 'together again' thing myself last night and it made me happy."

"So now is when you suddenly care about my happiness?" asked Colin.

"It's a little easier to do that when you actually *are* happy … so, yeah." she replied, "Is that a problem?"

"No, it's actually really …"

"Good, then let's get to it." Mary said, ending the moment before it could become too sincere.

****

Jack Anderson had the same "Let's get to it!" approach as Mary did while heading toward the same place, to meet the same person, for the same exact reason. The only difference was that he actually had possession of the trunk and was one key away from opening it. It was all thanks to his partnership with Nate Webster, who, like Colin, had begun having trouble buying into the spirited attitude. There was simply no room for it in a mind that could only think of his father's calls that he had been ignoring and the home he had not returned to in days.

As the Harbor Pointe bridge approached, Nate asked, "Are we going to this guy's house?"

"Well." Mr. Anderson replied, while thinking back to Charlie sharing his schedule over the phone.

2 days earlier

"I'm working every single day. I have no other option." Charlie said, "Saturday they even have me out on the actual beach ... the furthest thing from shade or air conditioning."

"You said Saturday?" asked Mr. Anderson.

"Yes."

"I could use some time on the beach." Mr. Anderson said, "I'll make my way over there then."

"You don't have to do that, sir."

"No, I really should. There's something I would like to discuss with you. I think you would be a big help to us, and, in return, we could be an even bigger help to you."

Chapter 13

The stoplight was just ahead. "Sir?" Nate asked after getting no response to his question.

"Oh, sorry." said Mr. Anderson, "Charlie basically lives at work, so that's where we'll meet him. We'll keep going straight." he said as he pointed at the Harbor Circle sign.

Colin and Mary were not too far behind; and when they eventually reached the same light, they made a left turn instead of going straight. Colin could not help but glance over at where he had been two nights before. Noticing the slew of cars around the bustling Harbor Circle, it could not have looked any more different. Among those cars, Mr. Anderson's car was parked. He and Nate had already started making their way to the beach.

The brutal sun beat down on them as they began to trek through the thick, hot sand. Nate, seeing someone to the side, asked, "What is he a lifeguard or something?" He was thinking of the limited jobs that could be done on a beach.

Mr. Anderson pointed ahead to an area with identical blue chairs spread out along the beach. "He works up there at the building." he replied. "It's a beach club. He's a server."

"Are you sure this guy is a part of the Webster family?" Nate asked wondering if he would be the one to wait on them.

Meanwhile, there were two other members of the Webster family who were doing quite a bit of waiting themselves at that same moment. Shortly after turning onto club drive, Mary's car came to a halt when it joined the long line of others waiting to get into the Harbor Pointe parking lot.

"What's the hold up?" asked Colin.

"You have to give your member number. I guess they are actually checking the list for it nowadays."

"Remember back when we would come and use Granddad's membership?" Colin said. "They'd just let you slide right on in. You would know it ... now that we don't actually have a member number to give, they're checking."

"Don't worry, I know one we can use." Mary said, remembering the one that Lee James had used the night before.

When it was their turn at the booth just ahead of the closed gate, the employee asked, "Member name and number?"

"James 22." Mary quickly answered.

"Guest?" asked the employee after seeing that Lee James had already checked himself in earlier.

"Yes." Mary confidently replied as if she belonged, "Two guests."

"Great. Have a nice day."

When the gate opened, she drove ahead into the parking lot. Colin couldn't stop himself from asking, "James? As in ..."

"Lee James." Mary said, "Do you remember him?"

"Oh yes, I do ... yes. I didn't know you guys were still together after all these years."

"We aren't ... well, we weren't. We were yesterday evening though ... here actually."

"So *that* was the 'together again' you were referring to?"

"You catch on quick." Mary replied.

Shortly thereafter they would both be catching on to multiple things, the first being that Uncle Charlie was nowhere to be found inside the clubhouse.

"If he isn't in here, then they either have him working at the pool or on the beach." said one of the other workers in response to their questioning his whereabouts.

Colin and Mary left the clubhouse and walked along the wooden deck toward the pool that was a short distance away. After opening the gate, they passed a restroom building before turning the corner to reach the pool.

"Wait." Mary said, stopping Colin. "I'll be right back. Don't make any kind of discovery without me."

"Okay." Colin replied as Mary walked into the restroom. "I guess I might as well go too."

Just as he reached for the men's restroom door handle, he heard the sound of beach music playing on the speakers. The voices and splashes in the pool enticed him just enough that he looked around the corner. He immediately wished he had never looked. The leisurely sight he had expected to see would have warmed his soul, but what he actually saw came closer to freezing it numb. A discovery had, in fact, been made. With it came an immediate second realization ... Lee James had not changed one bit. Still with the youthful look that Colin had remembered him wearing so well, Lee had been easily spotted in the pool ahead. What stole Colin's attention most was not only Lee's familiar look, but those who surrounded him.

A little girl screaming with joy landed in the water, apparently after Lee had tossed her in the air. Her small head popped up as she began to swim towards the edge of the pool where a woman with her legs in the water cheered her on. When the little girl passionately reached the woman's open-armed embrace, Lee stood a short way back and joined in the celebration. As he stood there clapping his hands, the shining smile on his face was no match for the glare of the bright shining sun which caught the glitter of a gold wedding ring on his left hand.

Does she know? Colin wondered about Mary. He certainly did not want any responsibility in ruining her newfound happiness with Lee. Colin, knowing he had a panicked mind that was hastily jumping to conclusions, internally asked himself, *Is that actually him?*

Colin's next thought was to just forget about both questions, turn around, and make a straight shot to the men's restroom. He would just pretend to have been there all along, and could act surprised when Mary saw what he had seen.

"No sight of him?" she asked Colin as he walked in her direction ... away from the pool.

The shock of what he had seen had left Colin almost numb. He couldn't say a word in response to her question. His pause allowed just enough time for Mary to glance beyond where her cousin stood and see her imagined future crumble before her very own eyes. When Colin saw the shocked look that suddenly washed over her face, he knew all that he needed to know.

The fact that Lee James had not changed one bit was something that Mary could also see for herself. Through her eyes, it went far beyond looks. She saw that his deceptive nature was still in full swing, and, the humbling feeling of being rendered useless came over her. Mary felt as though she had been thrown off the mountain top that had taken her so long to climb. The only thing Mary could bring herself to do was begin the painful search for another way up again.

Colin had not moved an inch from the moment that Mary entered the pool area. He could hardly bring himself to blink. Even after seeing his cousin turn around and head back in the opposite direction, Colin did not budge. Instead, with a statue-like stiffness, he shifted his eyes toward the sight that had pierced Mary's soul and realized it had gotten much worse.

Seeing the woman seated at the pool's edge wrapped up in Lee's arms, Colin said to himself, "Well, there's no way that *she* knows!"

Colin briefly wondered how Mary could possibly have passed on the opportunity to change that. He even wondered if he should do it himself, but he realized that was not his mission. He and Mary were in search of something big, and in order to find it, he had to make the same decision as Mary .... leave the scene instead of escalating it.

Colin noticed that Mary had already gained a considerable amount of distance as she briskly walked along the boardwalk in a way that did little to hide the turmoil she was experiencing. He followed Mary to the beach that she was approaching, making sure to give his cousin plenty of space while keeping his eyes focused on her as she walked among the crowd of people.

With his focus fully on Mary, he failed to notice Uncle Charlie seated in a beach chair facing Mr. Anderson, and Nate Brewer. Colin walked right past the three of them just as they began their discussion.

****

"Thank you for taking the time to do this." Mr. Anderson said to Charlie.

Charlie, just relieved to be on a break and able to sit down, replied, "Of course. Thanks for coming all this way. What is it that I can do for you?"

"First let me introduce … or I guess re-introduce you to Nate Brewer."

"Have we met before?" asked Charlie.

"Well, my father was married to your sister and …"

"Oh, I can hardly keep up with my own immediate family, so I wouldn't be able to connect all those dots. A lot has happened since those days, but it's good to see you."

"We think there's something you might have that we could really use. Do you remember receiving a vase that was handed down from your parents?" Mr. Anderson asked.

"A vase?" asked Charlie. "I really don't remember. What I do know is that my ex-wife has just about everything I owned. She'd be the one to ask. Heck, she had enough stuff to open up an antique business here in town."

"Interesting, we'll have to check that out when we leave." Mr. Anderson said to Nate.

"Why are y'all needing a vase? Have a bunch of flowers or something?" asked Charlie with a laugh.

"We need what's *inside* the vase."

"Water?" asked Charlie, continuing to find himself humorous.

"A key." Mr. Anderson said straight faced. "A key that could really solve a lot of your problems."

"Well then! I think I need that key. Let me know if you find it." said Charlie, still lacking any seriousness.

"Let's plan to meet later on." said Mr. Anderson, "When do you get off?"

"Six o'clock." Charlie replied, "Besides, what does this key open?"

"Let's meet at Captain Andy's restaurant, and I'll tell you there. Hopefully we'll know at that point. 6:15?" Mr. Anderson asked as he took out a small notepad from the back pocket of his pants. "Here, I'll write it down so you don't forget."

With a pen in hand, Mr. Anderson continued by asking, "And what was the name of that antique store?"

"Uhm … it's called Sea Treasures Antiques. It *should* be Charlie's Sea Treasures, but you know how it is."

"Clever name." said Mr. Anderson as he wrote it down. He then tore the slip of notepad paper with the restaurant name on it and handed it to Charlie.

"6:15 tonight. Alright? Don't forget." said Mr. Anderson.

Charlie replied, "I'll see you then."

Mr. Anderson and Nate walked back toward the Harbor Circle beach access, Nate, realizing that it was not even noon yet, asked, "Are we really going to stay here until 6:15?"

"I thought the cat got your tongue back there." Mr. Anderson replied, "But no … I've got something else in mind. Don't worry."

****

Similar to his former teacher, Colin's mind was also hard at work as he approached Mary. She had managed to find a spot on the beach away from the crowd of people and was seated in the sand facing the ocean. As he neared his distraught cousin, Colin felt around the inside of his pocket for the single sheet of paper that he had placed there at the last minute before leaving home that morning.

Colin sat down to the right of Mary. He sat there silently as he took a few moments to find the proper headspace to match the moment.

Speaking over the crashing waves, he began to speak without any idea of the direction that his words would lead.

"You know …" he said before letting the other voice inside of him take over … the same one that had told him to bring along the paper in his pocket.

"I don't think it's fair for me to have such good scenery." he continued.

Mary raised her head and faced Colin to ask, "What do you mean?"

"Well, it's been a long time; but, in the past when you talked me through a broken heart, all there was to look at was a bunch of soup cans, Now I have this awesome view."

Mary continued to look out at the ocean to the view of which he was speaking and replied, "Right … I remember that pantry. But look, you don't need to say anything. I'm grown now; this isn't middle school."

Colin replied, "You're right." He stood up and continued, "Take all the time you need. Just let me know when you're ready to go."

Mary nodded as Colin walked a short distance away from where he had been seated before reaching into his pocket again. With his right hand getting a hold on the paper, he balled it up and continued walking before that familiar internal voice broke through. It caused him to come to a sudden stop. He turned back around to look at Mary. With the balled-up paper in hand and out of his pocket, Colin walked closer and directly behind her. The appearance of Colin's shadow made his close proximity obvious to Mary. She could see his shadow on the sand and realized he had his hand up as if getting ready to throw something.

Mary turned to look at Colin and asked, "Dude, what are…?" She stopped short when she saw the ball of paper in the hand that was raised in a throwing position. "What are you doing?" Colin, after a brief pause, awkwardly replied, "I was going to throw this at you and say '*this* is middle school' but I'll just do this instead." He lightly tossed it to her.

Colin could see the extreme look of confusion on Mary's face. "Just open it and maybe it'll make sense." he continued. Mary looked at the ball of paper and straightened it out to see the words, "Colin and Mary Webster's Bucket List" written at the top of the page. The date on it was from over fifteen years before.

"Ah, this *is* middle school … I get what you tried to do there more so than what's on this little list. I can't believe you kept this."

"I couldn't just trash an incomplete list. Check number four."

Mary looked past the first three random bucket list items that included something about a parade, comedy routine, and finding the end of a rainbow. It was the letters "TBD" written after the number four that Colin referred to as making the list incomplete.

"Oh, right. I see" she said.

"So … I had a thought." said Colin, "We can do whatever that one thing is that you've always wanted to do. It can be anywhere and anything in the world … your choice."

"I don't know if I'm up for doing something like that today. But that's sweet of you, Colin. It really is."

"C'mon." he said, "This can either be a day where your heart was hurt by some jerk or it can be filled by experiencing something special. It's your choice."

Seeing that Mary was on the fence about his idea, Colin tried to nudge her over by continuing, "There's gotta be *something*."

"Well ..." Mary said before taking a pause, "... there is one thing."

That one thing that she had in mind was what led them back to Morriston. Just outside of the town, Mary approached a road sign with which she had struggled for quite a while. Every time she passed it, she could hardly bear to give it a simple glance. When she turned on that road, the destination became clear to Colin even though it was far from anything he could have imagined. Mary continued straight down the road to a dead end. A right turn exposed a sign that was just ahead.

It read, *"Morriston Town Cemetery"*

Colin, knowing that his cousin was vulnerably filled with emotion, spoke up, "Mary, what are you doing?"

"Something that's long overdue." she replied, "I've put this off long enough."

"Are you sure you want to do this?" he asked.

"I've never been more sure of anything in my life."

She parked the car and readily got out, leaving Colin seated in the passenger side. As she walked closer to the field full of gravestones, she stopped and turned back toward the car to get Colin's attention and signal for him to come with her.

After taking her key out of the ignition, Colin got out and walked to where she was waiting for him. "Are you sure you want me to come along?"

Mary was quick to say, "Colin, I'm positive. Without you I would have never even begun to think about doing this ... plus, I have no idea in which direction to go."

"I figured that was the case." Colin said, "Follow me."

Mary's heart pounded heavily as she delicately walked through the cemetery in anticipation of the closure that she so desperately craved.

"It's right up here." said Colin, hoping that it was in fact their grandparents' grave that she was wanting to see. It was easy to see that his assumptions were right after stepping out of the way to watch Mary slowly approach the gravestone in complete reverence.

After a brief moment of looking down at her grandparents' names carved into the headstone, Mary turned to Colin and asked, "Do you come here often?"

"I've only been a few times since her funeral." he replied before thinking about the one question that had been floating in his mind since that very event. It was that internal voice that turned those thoughts into words.

"Why didn't you go?" he asked, then adding unneeded clarification, "To the funeral?"

"The same reason I've avoided this place all of these years ... shame! I was ashamed of never being around for those last years of her life. I couldn't stand the fact that I had missed so much. To have that thrown at me all at once ... in one single day ... was too much to handle."

"And this right now isn't too much to handle?" he asked.

"If I was here alone, it probably would be ... but it's time."

With that said, an entirely different feeling wafted over Mary's spirit ... one that she gladly made the effort to catch. The overflowing abundance of relief that she felt, was restoring her battered spirit. A feeling of peace that she hadn't felt since she was very young filled her spirit.

As Colin stood there and watched the effect that this visit to their grandparents' graves had on his cousin, he realized that the most meaningful goal that they ever could have put on a bucket list was finally fulfilled. Mary could proudly say the same thing as well.

Chapter 14

Inside the Sea Treasures Antique Shop

Pointing upward toward the vase on the top of the shelf behind the checkout counter, the young girl working replied to Mr. Anderson's inquiry about a vase, "This is the only one we have."

"Okay. Would you mind if I take a closer look at it?"

"No problem." the girl said as she pulled out a step stool.

When the girl picked up the vase and carefully made her way back down the stool to place it on the counter, both Nate and Mr. Anderson could not help but notice the expensive price on the tag tied around the vase.

"Wow." Mr. Anderson said, pretending to show interest in the vase, "What a beauty!!"

What he really cared about was whether the key that he was deeply hoping would be taped to the inside of the vase would be there. He gently squeezed his hand inside it to feel around.

Giving the girl some explanation for his actions, he explained. "Just feeling around for any scratches. Very important."

Before saying anything more to him, the girl was distracted by a voice from a back room in the shop.

"Honey." the voice called.

"Yes, ma'am?"

"Come here for a second."

As the girl left the counter and headed to the back room, Mr. Anderson could feel nothing inside the vase. As he squeezed his hand back out, Nate asked, "Would it help if I did this?" He had already turned on the flashlight on his phone and was waiting to point it into the vase where Mr. Anderson's hand had just been.

"Maybe so, let's see." he replied just before he heard the same voice that he heard earlier from the store's back room ... only this time it was much closer.

"May I help you, sir?"

Mr. Anderson looked up to see a middle-aged woman directly in front of him with both hands on the counter. Coming face to face with her intimidating furrowed brow, he knew he needed to say something ... quick.

"No-no ma'am. I was just looking for-"

"This?" she asked, removing her right hand from the counter to expose a single key that had been covered by it.

"Uhm, well ... what's that for?" Mr. Anderson asked.

"I have no idea." she replied, "All I know is that it came from the same place where you were snooping. Even though it's a stretch to suggest this, I thought maybe you might know."

"What if I did?" he asked slyly.

"Well, if you really knew, then I would know too."

"Why is that?"

"Because." she said, holding up the key, "You would need this ... and in order to get this, you would have some explaining to do."

"Is it really yours, though?" Mr. Anderson asked.

Met with silence, he could tell immediately that his question had taken the lady off guard.

He continued, "Here's what I'm going to do. I'm going to write down a date, time, and place. Here's what you're going to do. You're going to bring your key to that place, at that time, and on that date." Nate watched in amazement as Mr. Anderson stated his plans with such a smooth sense of confidence while writing down on his pocket-sized pad of paper everything he had just said to her.

Jack Anderson tore the slip of paper off the pad and placed it onto the counter and, before making his exit, said to the lady, "I don't think I got your name."

"It's Janice."

"Great, Janice." Mr. Anderson replied as he slid the paper closer to her on the counter. "I'll see you soon, Janice."

"Let's roll." he said to Nate as he turned around to leave the store.

As soon as they walked back out into the heat of the day, Nate asked, "How can you be so sure that she'll show up?"

"She's intrigued." Mr. Anderson replied, "Janice is in there right now looking at that paper ... and she's realizing that I have the answers to something she's questioned for a long time. She'll be there, alright. He paused a moment before he added "... and she will not be the only one. That reminds me ... I have some calls to make."

Janice was indeed looking at the slip of paper with those exact thoughts. The interest did not come from the date Mr. Anderson had proposed. She noticed it was exactly two weeks away. Nor did the time that was set for 6:30 p.m. concern her. It was the location that drew her full interest.

****

Janice had no idea that she was looking at the exact same thing that a waitress from Captain Andy's restaurant was writing down as she held one hand on a similar sized notepad. With the phone resting between her ear and shoulder, she repeated the message that the man on the other line had told her to pass on to an incoming customer.

"Okay, just to clarify, August 28th, 6:30 p.m., Webster Inn. Is that all?" she asked.

Jack Anderson replied, "Yes, that's all. Pass that to the man wearing a white collared Harbor Pointe Beach club shirt. He should be getting there around 6:15. Then, if you could, write the same thing down for someone else. He should be there around the same time."

"Do you know what he'll be wearing?" she asked as she pulled out another slip of paper.

"No." Mr. Anderson replied, "But I have a feeling that he will eventually be seated beside the other guy that I mentioned."

****

Arriving at Captain Andy's several minutes before the "other guy" was the man that Mr. Anderson had referred to over the phone. He entered the restaurant during the height of the dinner rush and took a seat at one of the two empty booths where he was expecting his former teacher, Jack Anderson, to join him. While waiting, he wondered what had driven him to travel nearly an hour to Harbor Pointe Beach to meet Mr. Anderson.

Mr. Anderson had given him the impression that he had recently moved there since retiring and needed some consulting on a business plan he had in mind. He wondered if his former teacher was really that desperate for work opportunities or if he simply had too much time on his hands and wanted a last minute dinner partner. Each possibility was equally embarrassing in his mind. Nevertheless, he, Tony Webster, was there.

The other guy, Charlie Webster, had headed straight from work and arrived at the same restaurant expecting to meet Mr. Anderson. It was 6:18 p.m., and several minutes past their agreed upon time. Charlie walked in prepared to offer his apologies; but after scanning the busy restaurant, he saw no sign of Mr. Anderson. He did see two booths directly beside each other with open seats. One of those booths had an opened menu spread on the table and glass half full of water placed beside it. The other empty booth was closer to the main door, so he took a seat that he made himself comfortable there. Almost immediately after sitting down, a waitress came over with a menu and offered to take Charlie's drink order.

"Just a glass of ice cold water." he told her.

When she walked away, Charlie opened the menu and began scanning the various seafood options. It was then that Tony Webster left the restroom and made his way back into his booth which put him back to back with Charlie. He glanced at his watch after sitting down and saw that it was well past the 6:15 p.m. meeting time Mr. Anderson had set for them. Tony figured he would give it a few more minutes before checking in with him, so he picked up the menu and began to peruse all the offerings listed.

From behind the main counter, the waitress who had taken Mr. Anderson's earlier call spotted the man that met his description at the booth closest to the main entrance. She then looked over to the next booth to see another man. She thought to herself, *I guess that's what he meant.* Even though it was not exactly the image of two brothers sharing a table after spotting one another that Mr. Anderson had planned for, it was close enough.

The waitress approached the gentleman with the white collared shirt first. She felt absolutely sure one of the notes was for him.

"This is a message for you, Sir." she said before placing a slip of paper onto his table. As he pushed his menu aside to take a look at the note, she eased over to the next booth directly to her right. "Sir," she said to get his attention. Placing the note on the table in front of him, she said, "For you."

As both men were reading *August 28th, 6:30 p.m., Webster Inn* on the separate slips of paper, she was walking back toward her post at the main counter. She stopped short when she heard one of the men trying to get her attention. It was Tony … he had beaten Charlie to it.

"Ma'am?" he asked her. "Who is this from?"

Hearing the question from directly behind him, the first sign of familiarity in Charlie's mind came not from the voice, but from the question … it was the exact same one that he was about to ask.

Charlie listened for the waitress' response. "Some guy over the phone. I was not given a name." she replied.

Tony turned to face her. Still not realizing who was seated behind him, he asked, "What about mine?"

"Well, it was the same guy." she replied. "Identical message."

The voice of the man behind him broke in and said, "Tony?" It was a voice that he had not heard in a very long time. "Is that you?" the voice continued as the man in the next booth stood to his feet.

Seeing that her work appeared to be done, the waitress quietly excused herself. The message had officially been received.

Recognizing his brother, Charlie froze in position. "Tony?" Then his dry wit took over, "Tony … forgive me … I don't think I recall your last name."

The two men sat down … this time in the same booth. Tony, seated across from Charlie felt the surprising thrill of seeing his brother again.

"Only you could get away with a line like that." said Tony with a laugh.

Joining in on the laugh, but without any well-meaning, Charlie replied,

"The tension wasn't going to break itself."

"Right." Tony soberly replied, "It's uh- It's been awhile. How are things?"

"I think you know the answer to that." Charlie replied. "If you don't, you probably wouldn't want to know."

Quickly shifting gears, Tony asked, "I assume you were here to meet Mr. Anderson too?"

"Yeah. I wonder what this is all about." said Charlie as he held up the note.

Tony took another look at his slip of paper and replied, "There's no telling with that man. Are you going, though?"

"If the workplace allows for it, I guess so."

"I'm sure you have some seniority around there. They'll let you." Tony assumed.

"I just started." Charlie replied. Having given his brother a glimpse into his situation, he continued, "They have teenagers with more seniority than me. In fact, I was trained by one of them."

Tony realized there were no more gears to shift to with Charlie. He quickly understood why so much time had passed since their last encounter.

"Well." said Tony as he started to slide out from his side of the booth, "I need to get going, but I hope to maybe see you there in a couple of weeks." He then reached into his pocket and pulled out his business card. Handing it over to Charlie, he continued, "If you ever need anything, just give me a call."

"I appreciate that, but I'm not one for charity." Charlie replied, assuming that his brother was offering him help after hearing of his circumstances.

"It's not that, it's just to ..." Tony stopped himself from continuing. He made his final response simple, "I'll see you later." He wondered if "later" would ever come.

After watching his brother leave, Charlie looked at the number on the business card long enough to get past his sensitivity. He wondered if his brother really did have good intentions.

"Everything okay? Sir?" said another waitress. He had failed to notice that she was standing beside him to take his order.

"I'm sorry?" he asked.

"Are you okay?"

****

It was the same question that Mary pondered in her car outside of the Webster homestead that evening. She was there to drop off her cousin, Colin, after an eventful day together. It was he who had asked if she was okay.

"You know." she said, "For the first time in a while, I think I am."

Colin was left with a smile on his face as he watched her drive away. As he approached the house, he took out the cellphone that he had been ignoring throughout the day and saw four notifications on the screen … two missed calls and two voicemails that followed. One came from his boss, Tina Smith. The other, he did not recognize … not one he had saved in his contacts. It was that one he was interested in checking out first.

"Hey there. It's Amy. Amy Davis. I actually got this number from your boss at the Castwell Press. I hope you don't mind. There's just something I'd like to say to you. It's nothing related to your job, even though that's what I told your boss. Anyway, if you can, give me a call sometime soon. Preferably before the wedding rehearsal on the 26th."

When the voicemail ended, all Colin could think of was how little he had worked on his article about her wedding, which was less than two weeks away. Just before playing the other voicemail, Colin braced himself as he had a feeling that Tina Smith was thinking the same thing.

"Colin, I just received a call from Amy Davis, the girl you're supposedly interviewing. She wants your number, and I didn't think it was a good sign for her not to have it. I'd like to get an update on your progress thus far and-"

Colin ended the voicemail and hastened his steps into the house where he found his mother, Carolyn, on the phone. Before he could begin to make his way upstairs, she held up one finger as a signal for him to stop and wait for her to get off the phone.

"No, no. That's completely fine!" she said to the person on the line. "With our business, you probably could have made reservations two *days* in advance and it would have worked out. Two weeks is plenty of time to reserve every room."

"Every room?" Colin mouthed to her.

"Alright. It was good speaking with you, also." Carolyn said as the call neared its end, "We'll be in touch. Thank you!"

When she hung up, Carolyn responded, "*Every. Room.* And you'll never guess who that was."

"Who?"

"Mr. Jack Anderson!" she told him, "He said that he's planning a family reunion for that weekend and needs all our rooms for people to stay in!"

"Family reunion?" Colin asked, "I didn't think he had much family. They must be distant."

… The family that Mr. Anderson hoped to bring together had become exactly that … distant!

Chapter 15

Colin, after spending the better part of two weeks crafting various angles to his news article about the Harmony Acres Wedding Venue, had come to a dead end. The biggest part of the story had yet to be discovered, and, with the help of his boss, Tina Smith, he was quick to understand why.

She called him into her office after reviewing what he had pieced together. Looking up from the article he had sent her, she said, "I see a skeleton here. You have the bones, but there's no life in it." She paused briefly before asking, "Do you know why that is?"

"Well, I ... I, maybe because ..." Colin stammered.

"It has no heart." Tina broke in to say, answering her own question. "And do you know why it has no heart?"

Colin made no attempt to answer as she continued, "Because there's no mention of the actual wedding you're supposed to be covering. It's all about the venue which is fine, but that's not what people will expect to see."

"I understand that."

"Do you have any information at all about the wedding?"

"Well ...."

"Please tell me you've interviewed the couple."

Seeing the look on his face, Tina asked, "Did you at least get up with her after she asked for your number?"

Colin honestly responded, "Not exactly, but ..."

"But nothing!" she replied, "I suggest you better get around to it ... the

132

wedding is tomorrow! I don't know what you're waiting for."

She may not have known why he was putting off that part of the assignment, but Colin sure did. There was no way to forget about his impromptu beach excursion with Amy Davis. It had sparked a freeing feeling that he had never before experienced. With its freedom was a sense of captivity that came along with the addictive aura of Amy's intoxicating presence. That alone was what Colin had found himself immersed in after last seeing her on that memorable night. It was also what he hoped to avoid, especially as he recalled the long time it took to for him to recover from the tidal wave of adrenaline that had nearly drowned him. However, there was no getting around the fact that staying in that state of mind would not get the job done, even if it was in his best interest to do so.

He arrived at the Harmony Acres venue that evening for the wedding rehearsal with an "all-business" mindset. Even so, that would be tested from the get-go. With a voice recorder and legal pad in hand, the muffled sound of music from a car radio and the smell of smoke was all it took to divert him from his path to the wedding chapel where people were already gathered. Colin's eyes immediately were pinpointed toward a car he recognized well. As he got closer to it, the sound was louder and the smoke's odor heavier. Before he knew it, he found himself at Amy Davis' car window. It took a few hard knocks on the glass for her to realize he was there.

She quickly turned the radio volume all the way down and put out her cigarette. Sitting there in her luxurious leather seat, she rolled the window down. Colin could not help but cough as a flow of smoke from the cigarette was released toward him. With his head tilted, Colin leaned forward while he was still clearing his throat. The look on Amy's face was enough to tell him she was in a state of confusion.

"No." Amy said, as she slowly shook her head.

"No what?" asked Colin.

"You are the one who asked me. So now you have the answer ... No, I cannot marry him."

Colin tried to act as if he had no regard for her answer but it clearly had his mind topsy-turvy as he pointed toward the chapel and said, "Shouldn't you be ..."

"No." Amy was quick to say. "I can't. I just can't."

"Sure you can!" Colin desperately replied as he tried to keep his focus on the reason for him being there. "All you have to do tonight is just ..."

"No!" Amy interrupted him, He face was drawn and her eyes showed evidence of having been crying. "If I show up tonight ... then what about tomorrow night? It's really about tomorrow and, frankly, every other 'tomorrow' for the rest of my life."

A feeling of panic engulfed Colin. He stood there for a moment before he replied, "Oh, c'mon! Now's really not the time to think that far ahead. I mean, think about all of the planning you've done ... and Mary's hard work, the article, my *job*, and ..."

"Bruce." Amy said solemnly.

"Yes!" replied Colin, "and Bruce! Good 'ole Bruce. Can't forget him."

"No." said Amy as she looked past Colin and saw her fiancé walking toward her car. Her eyes were fixed on him as he neared the car.

As Colin turned to see what her eyes were fixed on, he saw him. "Bruce! Good 'ole Bruce." he said. His former classmate's arrival gave him such a sense of relief that he greeted him with a side hug.

"The newsboy!" he said to Colin before changing his tone.

"Hey Ames, sorry I'm late." he said. "Thanks for waiting for me. I would've looked really bad over there if I was the only one running behind."

It was obvious that Amy was in a very awkward position. She had thought that Bruce was already there. However, she went along with his assumption and timidly responded, "Oh, it's no problem. I guess we better get going."

Amy got out of the car slowly, pressed the lock button, and closed the door behind her. For a moment she locked eyes with Colin but then walked toward Bruce, and the two of them started toward where the crowd had gathered.

The only thing Colin could do was watch the two of them walk toward the chapel and wonder what he had just let happen. Left standing there on his own, the relief he had first felt when Bruce appeared had officially run dry. His discontent grew with every step in the other direction that the couple took. He had no choice but to follow them and was quickly called into action once he arrived at the chapel.

"Maybe he could do it." he overheard a voice say when he took his seat on the back row of the chairs that had been set out around the chapel.

Colin looked ahead to see his cousin, Mary, scrambling around and giving orders to the members of the wedding party. He knew she was in her element, and it was the first sign that he had possibly done the right thing to encourage the wedding to proceed as planned. As Colin began jotting down a few notes, he heard the same voices once again.

"Ma'am." one of them said to Mary, "Could that gentleman over there do it?"

Colin looked up to see a finger pointing directly at him while, at the same time, Mary started to walk toward him.

"Hey, hi." she said in a chaotic manner, "The family is desperate to have a stand in for the minister. Would you *please* be willing to go up and do that?"

"Oh, I don't know." Colin replied. He could just visualize himself standing in between the couple, the exact thing he had hoped to avoid.

All it took, though, was one desperate plea from Mary to cause him to comply with her request. He reluctantly set his legal pad and pen aside and made his way up to the chapel's platform. There was nothing to the task he had been asked to do … other than the looking straight ahead and pretending that the intense tension between himself and Amy did not exist. She managed to do the same thing until an unthinkable action took place in the middle of the rehearsal. It was then that there was no more pretending.

"I just can't wait any longer." Bruce whispered to Amy before repeating himself loud enough for everyone else to hear. "I have to do this now … I must!" he said as he walked down from the platform.

Mary came near from where she was standing in the back with obvious displeasure at the interruption. She really felt that Bruce had no right to make his voice heard this late into the planning stages, "What is it?" she asked him.

"The song." he said in a manner that indicated there had been a prior discussion about it.

"Oh! The *song*." she said, remembering to what he was referring. "Now?? Are you sure?" she asked him with concern, "What about the surprise in the *actual moment*?"

"I'm positive. The moment is now." Bruce replied before turning to his groomsmen to say, "Wheel it on out here boys! We're doing this."

He looked over to Mary who needed no words to express her confusion and explained, "You know how you put me in charge of the music because it would be the one thing that I wouldn't screw up?" Seeing her nod, Bruce continued, "Well ... I took matters into my own hands ... literally."

By that point two of the groomsmen were struggling to wheel over a large object with a black cover over it. A few of the other guys joined to give them a hand. Until they got to the chapel area, everyone else knew nothing of the surprise. They tried to imagine what could possibly be under the cover. The first thought that most of them had was a piano, but it was quickly ruled out when they really thought about it. They knew Bruce Williams could not possibly be associated with such a thing. There was a higher likelihood that it might be some crazy portable bar that happened to play music ... they could easily see that pairing.

Colin paid no attention to what was approaching the chapel, his focus was on the people who were already there. He was observing Amy's look of wonderment at Bruce's nervous sense of excitement. He knew that was a side of her fiancé that she did not see often.

There was no dramatic unveiling of the object. Bruce simply walked over to it and removed the black cover to expose the vintage piano that was beneath. Once he tossed the cover aside, he pulled over a chair and took his seat behind the keyboard. He then began to give some context to his activity in the months leading up to that day.

"This is my great-grandmother's piano. I planned on restoring it to put in our home, but then I figured that it might as well be used. Mary, as soon as you mentioned 'music' to me, I could hear the sounds of our own children playing and singing at this piano. For some crazy reason, I could see myself sitting with them doing the same thing."

Colin, like all the others around the chapel, had been hanging on to Bruce's every word before he took another look at Amy and could see the tears welling up in her eyes.

They had no choice but to overflow and stream down her face when Bruce continued, "Just like the thought of you becoming my wife, it was a thing of beauty. I knew that I would do whatever it took for it to become reality."

They all had an idea of what was coming, but the moment that Bruce put his fingers on the piano keys and began to sing his rendition of Nat King Cole's song "That's All," everyone seemed to be overcome with emotion ... even Colin. However, as he was maintaining the role of an onlooker, his feelings were coming from a different place. Standing at the highest point on the chapel's front platform, he could see his cousin, Mary, standing behind the members of the wedding party. In reaction to the moment that reminded Mary of her purpose for committing herself to that job, a look of pride came on her face as she removed the tissue with which she had dabbed her moist eyes.

Through Colin's lens, the experience did not culminate with the song's ending but the realization that he had discovered the heart of a story worth sharing in his news article.

August 27th - Wedding Day

Colin arrived at Harmony Acres before any of the guests. He needed only one more thing for his article. For it to be complete, a picture of the couple's first official kiss as husband and wife was a must. That moment was to be captured with the camera dangling over his tie. Printed on the camera strap that hung around Colin's neck were the words, "Property of Castwell Press." After taking his seat on the back row in the chair closest to the aisle, Colin placed the camera on the seat next to him. He wiped the sweat, which the hot summer afternoon had caused to form, from his forehead. Then he unbuttoned his shirt sleeves and rolled them up. Exposing his wristwatch showed him exactly how early he was.

As he sat there, the only thing on his mind was a recap of the evening before and everything that it had entailed. The wedding rehearsal had turned into one big family sing along session which Bruce's piano presentation had set off. It had presented another hurdle for Colin and had delayed his newly found inspiration from being typed into his home computer. Instead, his ideas had been scribbled down on his legal pad while he waited patiently for the rehearsal to resume. Mary sitting beside him was the only reason he had not got up and gone home.

Knowing that things were completely off schedule, he had asked her, "Are you going to say something?"

"You know what? I think I should." she replied before she had stood up from her seat. "Hey, guys!" she yelled over to them.

The piano playing came to a stop in mid-song, as did the collective voices of everyone singing. They all looked over to Mary and some even headed back to their places, figuring it was back to business just as the serious expression on her face had suggested.

"I hate to do this, but … for the next song you are all going to have to hear this voice of mine whether you like it or not."

They had all let out a cheer and picked up where they had left off in their song, Mary had sat back down and continued enjoying the show they were putting on.

In response to her tactics that had fooled him more so than anyone else, Colin asked, "What was that about?"

"You know that phrase, 'if you can't beat them, join them,'? Well, look at that sight up there." she had said to him.

Colin remembered looking ahead and seeing an image of happiness in its purest form. It was a sight that he had been without long enough for it not to jade him. The couple's joyful expressions while their hands were locked together had symbolized what love was all about. He realized in that moment that every person deserves a chance to find new life and breath.

Mary had watched Colin take it all in and continued, "I mean, you can't beat that." She stood up once again and asked him, "So, would you like to join?"

Colin had only smiled as he was getting up to join the fun from the very seat he was back sitting in now. It had led to a very late night and had concluded with a finished article that had basically written itself. As a result of the late night before, he felt another yawn coming on. He checked his watch again and wondered why exactly he had gotten there so early.

Eventually, a car could be heard rolling up to one of the cottages behind where Colin was seated. He turned around to see Bruce, along with all of his groomsmen, pile out of the suburban vehicle and into the building. They were each, in zombie-like fashion, carrying their rented suits on hangers. From the looks of it, a whole other party had obviously occurred after the one Colin had experienced. It was not too long after they had all dragged in that they emerged from the cottage in their matching suits. They looked as if they had suddenly gone through a magic recovery. It was clear they had experienced that a time or two before and were ready to do it all over again.

Also showing signs of the late night before was his cousin, Mary. Colin marveled at her ability to direct all of the moving parts of the ceremony into the right direction. Much of the event's seamlessness had to do with the two people around whom it was centered. It was their relationship that had seemingly been reborn into something fresh that each and every one there could witness and wish for in their own lives. When Bruce and Amy met at the altar, Colin looked into his camera and zoomed in to prepare for the shot that he needed to capture. It gave him the clearest and most intimate view of two people that had fallen in love all over again right before his very own eyes.

Colin could do nothing except submit to the powerful forces of the emotions that he had never wanted to experience. There was simply no way he could beat them, and like the night before, Colin was left with only one thing to do … join them. In response to his high emotions, he began to paint over the stereotyped image in his head that had always made such thoughts inconceivable to him. With a clean slate, Colin was able to hope for a new image in which he could include himself … one that was nearly identical to what he was taking in through the lens of the camera.

When the guests rose to their feet and cheered for the couple after they were pronounced husband and wife, Bruce held up his hand that was locked with Amy's and victoriously said, "Thank you! Thank you all."

It was the perfect photo opportunity for Colin as he continued to look into the camera in hopes of getting one extra shot. With several people in the way, he moved further into the aisle until he got a clear view of the bride and groom. It was then that he saw Amy focusing directly in his direction with a deep stare into the camera. The extra picture was no longer important to

Colin ... he wanted to experience the moment with his own eyes. He lowered both hands that gripped the camera. Once it was removed from his path of vision, he saw Amy mouthing the words, "Thank *you*."

He was given no time to react or respond in any way before feeling a tap on his shoulder. Colin turned to see Mary tilting her head toward the direction where he had been seated with a look on her face that said, "*You're in the way.*" Once Colin stepped aside, Mary began waving for Bruce and Amy to step down from the platform and come toward her as the sound of joyous music played on the speakers. While the guests clapped their hands to the up tempo beat, the wedding party procession began dancing their way back down the aisle. Colin paid none of them any mind as they each passed by. Instead, he watched Mary, the one who guided them all along.

A song much different from what everyone else was hearing was filling his mind. Its solemn tone was raised to higher levels as the sweet feeling of seeing the job at its completion quickly turned bitter. It was a new form of normality that washed over him reminding him of the very things he had lacked in life. As a result, Colin let himself grow accustomed to a fleeting routine that was on the cusp of its moment of expiration. His inner song's tempo continued on a constant decline while he tried to savor every last bit of a story that was coming to a bittersweet end. While those around him followed Mary's lead to the reception tent, Colin understood that he had gone as far as he could possibly go ... The song was officially over.

Chapter 16

Lying flat on the mattress with his eyes fixed on the attic bedroom's wooden ceiling, Colin aggressively took deep breaths in and out. He had been forced to come to grips with his relationship with his special cousin. Colin reckoned with the idea of having to enter that fight once again. Was this really a reason for him to pick up the phone and give Mary a call? Because straight thinking was hard to come by at that moment, Colin had no way of knowing. Heightening his disgust and blocking his train of thought was the repetitive thumping noise that came from something being thrown against the small attic window near the roof. Colin got up from his bed and stomped over toward the window. Once he cleared the thick cobwebs around the sill, he struggled to push it open.

"Listen here!" Colin yelled out while squeezing his head through, "I thought I told you to…" He suddenly grew silent as he recognized someone very different from whom he had initially suspected.

"You thought wrong." said Mary in reaction to Colin's perplexity which came across very clearly as she looked up at him. With her arm cocked back in preparation to yet again throw the small stick that was in her hand, Mary continued, "I was getting tired of having to do this."

"Yeah. As you can tell, I was getting tired of it too." he said with a feeling a remorse, "I just thought you were…"

"I thought you had a phone! No?" asked Mary. She had called him several times over the past hour in reaction to a gathering of which Colin was still unaware.

"Oh, sorry. I have a tradition of completely ignoring it on most weekends. There's usually not much to miss … especially after just completing a work assignment."

"Well, you're definitely missing something today."

"Wait, so you came all the way here because I didn't pick up the phone?"

Mary replied, "No, that's why I started chucking this stick. I was already here."

Colin looked toward the front circular driveway but saw nothing. The cars were parked at an angle that Colin could not see from his window. She continued, "And I'm not the only one."

Over an hour earlier

"I don't know about this." Nate Brewer said to Mr. Anderson as he was stopping the car just after turning into the Webster Inn driveway.

"Oh, you'll be fine." Mr. Anderson calmly replied with a hand on Nate's shoulder.

Pointing back at the storage trunk in the backseat, Nate asked, "You expect me to just walk in there after taking something so valuable from them?"

"I expect you to trust the plan. Plus, we're giving it, and hopefully so much more, back to them right now. So let's go!"

Given the role model his father had been, Nate had trust issues — but the idea of trust was easy for Nate to accept when it came to Mr. Jack Anderson. It was his lead that he had been following. It was his spare bedroom that he could call home, and it was his presence that had become a refuge for Nate's lost soul. In one single moment, Nate knew how far this plan had taken him and how much his life was changing because of Mr. Anderson. He willfully shifted the car back in gear and continued on toward the front circular driveway. He slowly pulled up to where the passenger door was aligned with the sidewalk that led to the front entrance.

"Wait in here until I turn and give you a signal to get out." Mr. Anderson said.

"Gladly." Nate said as Mr. Anderson opened the car door, got out, and walked toward the house. Nate was fighting an urge that once would have easily defeated him … the urge to drive away and never come back. It was a victory for Nate to turn the engine off and take the key out of the ignition … one for which he could credit his past and present teacher. Mr. Anderson rang the doorbell and patiently waited for the door to be opened. When it finally was, Jack Anderson took in the admiration that he was used to receiving from others with much appreciation.

"Look who it is!" Carolyn said, "Mr. Anderson, it's so good to see you!"

"Likewise, my dear. How are you doing? It's been quite a while."

"I'm well. Your call about this reservation definitely gave me a boost!"

"I'm glad to hear that."

"Oh, and congratulations on your retirement. I'm sure this time of year has felt strange without the preparations for a new school year."

"Well, I thought that would be the case, but thankfully I've been preoccupied with a new challenge as of late."

"And planning your reunion, I'm sure, has also kept you busy." Carolyn added.

"That's actually been the new challenge, and I must say, it's not 'my' reunion." Mr. Anderson said before turning to face his car and signaling Nate to come in.

Nate took his cue, as well as a deep breath, while getting out of the car. Mr. Anderson turned back to see that Carolyn was back inside the house calling for her son.

"Colin! Would you mind coming down to assist Mr. Anderson with his things?"

"Oh, no I only have one thing that needs …"

"He's coming right down."

"Actually…" Mr. Anderson tried to say more before looking back at Nate who had his arms out and wondered what to do next. Jack Anderson had no answers to give him as he too held out his arms and turned back to see Colin walking toward him.

"There he is! Welcome! It's good to see-" Colin began, but came to an immediate stop with both his words and steps just before reaching the porch.

"What is this?" he asked.

"Nate." said Mr. Anderson, "Can you grab what's in the backseat for me?"

"*Nate?*" Carolyn thought when she heard the name spoken. She quickly moved from behind where Colin was standing. Seeing that it was Nate Brewer, she said, "I know who that is!" Her voice sounded much different from the disdainful tone of her son. The conversation continued when, after seeing the trunk that Nate took out of the car, Colin said, "I know **what** that is."

Carolyn could see for herself what Nate was holding as he stood before them. He had managed to keep his eyes focused on the ground.

"What's going on?" she asked.

Recognizing how close his plan was to becoming unhinged, Mr. Anderson pleaded, "Let me explain things."

"Please do." said Colin, "I'd like to know how you convinced that *thug* to return a stolen item face to face."

"Stolen?!" Carolyn exclaimed, "You didn't tell me that!"

"What's there to tell? He took what he came to get and left. It wasn't worth the trouble."

"But it was." said Mr. Anderson. "It was worth every bit of trouble. That's why I told him to take it."

"You … You are unbelievable … or should I say … *believable*." Colin said as he began to clap his hands. "Bravo, what a performance. A true mastermind."

When Jack Anderson saw Colin leave the porch and storm back into the house, he made no effort to explain the plan that was now putting his ethics into question. Carolyn also chose to leave, though in a less dramatic fashion than her son. Being the one who was more likely to hear another person out, she faced Mr. Anderson one more time to get some clarification.

"So, you aren't a part of any reunion, are you?" she asked.

Mr. Anderson shook his head and replied, "I'm not, no."

"Thought so." said Carolyn, reaching for the handle on the front door that Colin had slammed shut. While she was adding yet another thing to her laundry list of setbacks, Mr. Anderson spoke up once again.

Hearing something from behind where he stood, Mr. Anderson glanced down at his watch to see the time. *6:24 p.m.* It led him to confidently say, "But you're a part of one. Right now, actually."

He had caught Carolyn just as she was closing the door and struck a nerve within her that gave her no choice but to respond. Taking his words as those of a smart aleck, Carolyn closed her eyes to collect her thoughts before turning around to say, "Listen here, you have no ..." Just at that moment she was distracted by the sound of another car driving into the driveway. She heard a car door slam and looked out to see who it was. Getting out of that car was Tony Webster, who, after opening the passenger door to let out his wife, smiled and pointed at Jack Anderson as he approached.

"You sly dog!" he said, impressed with the former teacher's successful strategy to bring him back to his homeplace.

With a laugh, Mr. Anderson replied, "I'll be sure to remember who got here first between you and your brother. He is coming, right?"

Just as he finished his sentence, the back door of Tony's car opened and out stepped Charlie Webster. He spoke up and said, "Oh, he came!"

"Well, look-a there!" Jack Anderson declared with expressions of boundless joy flooding him all at once. "Everyone's first!"

"A close second will be my three girls." said Tony, "They're on the way. I wanted them to come back and see the old stomping grounds."

"That's perfect." said Mr. Anderson.

Charlie asked, "Did you ever get my key back from Janice? I'm sure she had it."

"She did ... does. But hopefully *you* will be getting it back shortly. I'm expecting her to show up."

"So the success of this whole get together depends on whether or not she'll show up? Ha! Well, it was a good try." Charlie said, acting as if he was about to get back into the car.

"Oh now c'mon. Let's try to think positively." Mr. Anderson said, "How about let's all go inside." Turning, he saw Carolyn; and, he saw Nate holding the trunk.

The moment Carolyn saw her brothers appear, she felt a sense of urgency to do something other than stand there and wait for them to walk up.

Nate Brewer, holding the trunk with both hands, was between her and the vehicle that Mr. Anderson, her brothers, and sister-in-law were standing near. He remained there with his face downward and silent while the others held a conversation. Over their conversation, he suddenly heard the sound, "Psst." coming from the other direction. When Nate looked over toward where the sound came from, he saw Carolyn beckoning him closer to where she stood. Before doing so, he bent over to put the trunk down.

With it inches away from touching the ground Nate heard her say, "Bring it!"

While Mr. Anderson was distracted with welcoming the first group of the Webster family, Nate swiftly approached Carolyn and was led inside of the house. She closed the front door behind her and was back in guest preparation mode — one quite different from how she prepared for her usual guests.

Nate began, "Look, I sincerely apologize for-"

"Thank you, but there's no time." Carolyn said, "Here's what's going to happen. I need you to place that trunk over in the sitting room. I'll grab a tablecloth to match its color. Make sure it's front and center and maybe open it up a little bit."

When it was set up to her liking, Carolyn continued, "Now that your hands are free you can help me prepare some drinks and snacks."

Within a few minutes, her orders had produced quite the presentation for her family to enjoy upon entering the house. From the looks of it, Tony and Charlie saw no signs of the meeting being unexpected by their sister. Both seemed very appreciative of Carolyn's efforts to welcome them. However, something still felt out of sorts for all three siblings. For the brothers, though it was like walking into a time capsule that stored years' worth of memories, the place did not feel like home. The nostalgia began to wear off as the three siblings sat there on the couches arranged in the same spots as they had always been. They each desperately searched their minds for the perfect subject of discussion but conversation was minimal.

Silence ensued as everyone stared at the opened trunk with three key holes lined up vertically. Two of the keyholes had keys placed in them. As they sat there in what felt like a waiting game for the last key, the outcome seemed increasingly doubtful as the minutes slowly passed.

"Are you sure she's coming?" Tony asked Mr. Anderson.

As a man who was used to having all of the answers, Mr. Anderson found himself feeling a little more unsure. All he could say was, "Well, we can only hope."

Nate Brewer spoke up, "I'll have to say, his pitch was convincing. If I was her, I would be here."

"Who is this guy?" asked Charlie before the ringing doorbell sound made him instantly toss his question aside. Everyone in the room immediately stood up from their seats.

Mr. Anderson took charge. He briskly approached the front door and opened it to see three young ladies.

"Hey there, are you with Janice?" he asked them.

"No." Tony begrudgingly said from behind him before a stern look from his wife made him lighten up, "They're my three daughters. Come on inside, girls. You haven't missed anything yet ... anything at all."

While the three young ladies walked through the doorway, Mr. Anderson recognized the two of them he had taught. Mary Webster was one of them. Before getting too far, she was pulled aside by Carolyn.

"Mary, Hi. It's been such a long time since I have seen you." She quickly changed the conversation to say, "Look, would you mind going upstairs and trying to convince Colin to come down? I think you're the only one he would consider listening to right now."

Ten minutes later

Colin had indeed listened to his cousin Mary who had convinced him to leave the upstairs living area. After opening the door, he looked over the second floor hallway balcony and could see the main sitting room below where the others were gathered. His thoughts were all over the place. He almost felt that he had been transported back to a different period of time.

What the- How the- Colin thought to himself before realizing that he was not going to find his answers to the "what" and "how" from a distance ... he needed to get into the thick of it. As he took his first step down the staircase, the sound from the sitting room seemed to reach its climactic point. It was not because those waiting in there saw him approaching, though. It was the sound of that familiar doorbell ringing once again. Everyone felt sure it would be Janice at the door, but Carolyn quickly pulled the emergency brake.

Once everyone stood up from their seats and Mr. Anderson began to walk over to the door, Carolyn used her voice of reason and said to them, "I think it's just Mary. She stepped outside a few minutes ago."

Just as they had stood up at the same time, everyone remained in sync with the sigh that came before their attention was called to the other side of the room.

"*Just* Mary is over here."

They turned around to see Mary. Without knowing that she had re-entered through the garage door, Carolyn's credibility withered away. Left feeling both mystified and slightly embarrassed, she quickly brushed herself off after Mr. Anderson continued in his pursuit toward the front entrance and opened the door. Colin had retracted his lone step on the staircase; and, from where he stood by the upstairs window, he could see the property's front driveway. With that view, he already knew what everyone downstairs was soon to find out.

Chapter 17

When the door flung open and Janice was not the person standing there, the roller coaster of anticipation that the Webster family was riding dropped to its lowest point. Charlie seemed to handle the fall better than the others. While the others were experiencing the obvious disappointment of it not being her, he explained, "Well, I saw this one coming."

Mr. Anderson had lowered his head as he saw the girl standing in the doorway; but after a moment, he looked up at her and said, "Please tell me you know someone named Janice."

"Why, Yes I do." she replied, "I work for her."

The anticipation of the roller coaster ride re-emerged in those waiting, and the excitement grew higher as she reached inside of her purse and took out a white envelope.

"She told me to drive *all* the way out here to give this to Jack Anderson."

"That's me. I'm Jack Anderson." he said with his hand held out toward her.

"It feels like there's hardly anything in this, but here you go." she said while handing over the envelope.

Mr. Anderson unsealed the envelope to see the brass key inside. He recognized it immediately as the same one he had laid his eyes on inside Janice's antique shop. He took it from the envelope to take a closer look. He slid his finger down from the key's shoulder and along its ridges. With the final obstacle evidently behind him, the feeling was actually less satisfying than he imagined it would be. There was something about it that did not feel rewarding, and the sudden simplicity of it all left him with discontent. He wondered if he had overestimated the end result of his plan that had seemed so perfect in his mind. Shifting his eyes away from the key, he saw that the young lady was already halfway back to her car.

"Wait." Mr. Anderson said as he stepped out on the front stoop to get the girl's attention. There were several newly formed questions to which he wanted answers. "Why didn't Janice bring this herself?"

"Busy I guess." the girl said, "I don't know."

"So that's it? She didn't want any part of this? She didn't want anything in return?"

"She didn't say that she did. She really didn't seem to care much about it."

When Jack Anderson turned to go back inside, he nearly ran into a wall of Websters after they had inched their way closer and closer to him. Speaking for the entire family, Tony asked, "Is that the one?" Unconvinced and with more doubt than anyone else there, Charlie replied, "I wouldn't bet too much on it."

Mr. Anderson had plenty of his own misgivings about what would come next, but he realized that to make sense of Janice's sudden disinterest in the key would require an attempt to place the key in the trunk's middle keyhole.

The Webster family cleared the way for him to pass through, and followed him inside to the opened trunk, there was no question that a new tone had been set. They were all anxious to see if the key fit. Without any unnecessary dramatization, as Mr. Anderson seamlessly inserted the key. He turned it as if he was unlocking the door to his own home. While doing so, Mr. Anderson could feel the breaths of the family members huddled behind him as they leaned forward as one collective body.

"It fits." he nonchalantly said to them, causing a release of their intensified levels of pleasure. The tight huddle broke apart with sounds of jubilation until they heard a voice coming from upstairs break up the premature celebration.

Looking up, they saw Colin leaning against the ledge on the second level. He was looking directly toward the trunk.

"What's inside of it?" Colin asked.

At the sound of his voice, the members of the Webster family seemed to

150

sober up from the mania of triumph by which they had been intoxicated.

With a level head, Mr. Anderson spoke up in an authoritative manner, "Let's all just calm down and keep order." He was pulling on the small knob, that, having been shut for years, required both hands to open. He needed Tony and Carolyn to hold the trunk still on the small table where it had been placed while he yanked on the door in a tug-of-war fashion.

Charlie, tired of watching him struggle, said to Mr. Anderson, "Here, let me take a crack at it." Mr. Anderson welcomed his offer and moved aside. Charlie, seemingly without any trouble at all, proceeded to open the door.

Feeling relief at the door being opened, Jack Anderson thought to himself, *He's lucky I loosened it up.* He watched the family immediately gather over the trunk. He didn't get a chance to satisfy his own curiosity as to what it was in the trunk that was meant to bring the "family together again." What he saw in their demeanor seemed to be the opposite of that goal.

One by one, the Websters slowly moved away from the trunk. That made room for Mr. Anderson to see twelve Christmas ornaments that had been placed in a styrofoam protector. They were of various sizes but in no particular order. Each of the ornaments was representative of the objects in the song, *The Twelve Days of Christmas.* It had been a family tradition to sing that song each Christmas Eve when the family gathered to celebrate. They were arranged in the order they were mentioned in that song. A single partridge in a pear tree was the first and smallest among the others. Taking up the most space was an ornament of twelve drummers in marching uniforms.

Though Mr. Anderson marveled at the exquisite detail in each ornament, he too was a bit underwhelmed and sought out some context by asking, "Does this mean anything?"

"It means that Mom got the last laugh." Tony said. He then looked up to the sky and continued, "Good one, Mom!" Then he turned to the other family members, and said, "Are you ready to go?"

All of them but one nodded and headed in the same direction from which they had entered. Mary started to follow them but broke away from her two sisters and walked back to the opened trunk to take a second look. Mr. Anderson stepped aside as she reached for the second smallest ornament and removed it from the protector. It was as if a replay button had been pressed in her mind when she saw the two turtle doves attached together. She was remembering the part she and Colin had shared in that song during the family celebrations. All those years growing up together and singing that part was all she could think about as she held the ornament tightly in her hand. With the hope that her cousin felt the same way, Mary looked to the upstairs ledge only to see that Colin was no longer there.

Moments earlier, while the rest of the family was experiencing a defeated feeling from the lack of anything exciting in the trunk, Colin had happened to notice Nate slip out of the sitting room just after the trunk had been opened. Nate was in no way alienated from the disappointment when he realized the life-altering plan he had undertaken appeared to have produced mediocre results.

Nate had walked outside for a moment alone. He was standing with his back facing the house against the driver's side of Mr. Anderson's car. The solemnity of the moment was cut short when Colin, from behind him, said, "The air isn't as tight out here, is it?"

Nate shook his head in agreement, but he was experiencing a suffocating feeling that he suddenly felt upon seeing Colin approach him.

"Curve balls are pretty hard to hit." said Colin, "In times like this, it's the ball that does all the hitting."

"Are you trying to say that you're the curve ball that's about to actually hit me?" asked Nate, "If so, I don't blame you. I deserve it."

"No." Colin replied. He had now realized that Mr. Anderson's intended end goal was pure. He continued, "I think you've already been hit hard enough … all of us have been. That ball is going to leave a bruise on all of us, but it'll eventually fade away. We'll get over it." He didn't realize that the bruise would grow darker and more painful before any healing could take place.

Inside of the house, the ridicule was evident. However, Carolyn took the opportunity to jump into the conversation in order to give Mr. Anderson her perception of what the mystery of the trunk had meant as she said, "It was Mom's way to bring us together in one room again. She truly loved nothing more."

Tony scoffed, "Here we are … in one room. Mission accomplished. This sure was fun and was *totally* worth the trip."

"I think Janice got the last laugh too. I remember her helping Mom put together some special presentation before what would have been her last Christmas. She never told me what it was or anything. Guess we had to find out the hard way."

"The joke's on us." Tony added.

"Oh yeah. She knew it wasn't worth the risk to come when she thought of the possibility of this happening. She stayed put in Harbor Pointe. I should've done the same thing." said Charlie.

As the brothers walked toward the door, Tony said, "Now I've gotta drive you all the way back there."

"Maybe that young chick is still around to give me a lift." Charlie said, only to see that her car was gone when the door was opened.

"Nope." Tony said, "She was a step ahead of us."

"Wait a second!" Carolyn demanded, causing them to stop before walking outside, "What 'joke' are you talking about? I'm not seeing any jokes here."

Charlie began to laugh while saying, "It's pretty funny, actually." His maddening laughter grew, "We really thought that we'd be set for life once that thing was opened up."

Carolyn's feelings intensified when she saw Tony join in on the mockery by saying, "Don't be so hostile with your guests, Sis. I wouldn't want to leave a bad review for your inn."

Following her brothers outside the house, she stomped closer to them and said, "You aren't guests! This is supposed to be *our* home!"

"But yet you're living in it." Tony dryly replied.

Before Carolyn could go any further or say anything else, she was stopped from doing both when Mr. Anderson grabbed her arm and said to her, "Your job is done."

They both watched Tony's car drive away. Soon the horn sounded from the smaller car that had been parked behind Tony's, and Mary placed the ornament back in the trunk and rushed outside to join her two sisters. Colin remained next to Mr. Anderson's car and observed everyone make their abrupt exits. Seeing Mary brush past his mother on the porch and jog toward her sister's car, Colin knew he could no longer remain still. Approaching her direction, Colin spoke up, "Hey!" He realized that she would have never thought to look for him if he said nothing.

Mary slowed her pace and said, "Hi. Look, I-"

"Let's go!" yelled her sister from inside the car. She already had the motor running.

"Hold on!" Mary responded. Turning back toward Colin, just as her mouth opened to speak again, her phone's ringtone beat her to the punch. When she took a look at the screen, her finger swiped across it. When Mary held the phone up to her ear it wasn't "Hold on" that she said through the speaker … it was, "Hello? Yes, this is Mary. From Harmony Acres, yes … Oh, Hi! It's good to hear from you again."

After seeing Mary hold up one finger as a signal for him to stand by, Colin took it more as a goodbye. He willingly made the choice to accept it as such. He walked toward the front porch where his mother stood next to Mr. Anderson.

Seeing Colin sluggishly walking closer, Mr. Anderson told Carolyn, "Sometimes all we can do is plant a seed and hope that it grows."

Epilogue

Over 3 Months later. Thanksgiving Day.

"You haven't even touched your food, Darling." Tony's wife said to him while they sat around the dining room table where they were joined by their three daughters.

Picking up his fork for the first time after staring off into the distance, Tony replied, "Oh, right."

"What are you thinking about?" she asked him.

His answer remained unspoken.

****

Charlie Webster, sitting in his recliner with a full stomach while the football game on television played in the background, held his brother's business card in one hand and his cell phone in the other. The number was entered for the second time ever on his phone's dial pad, but before pressing the green "call" button, Charlie held down the backspace key until the number was no longer there.

****

Jack Anderson, seated at his kitchen bar with a plate of half-eaten pie pushed aside, reached for the two binders stacked beside his landline phone. He removed the top one that was filled with the contact information for many of his former students. He pulled out the bottom one with "Anderson family" written on its dust-filled cover. Mr. Anderson opened up the binder; and after

155

scanning the single row of names, addresses, and phone numbers, he grabbed a pin from his shirt pocket. Once he marked through the names of deceased family members who had passed long ago, he was left with only one name, address, and number. Unsure if his nephew even knew he existed, Mr. Anderson nearly placed the binder in the nearby trash can. However, he put it back in its spot instead. Fully aware of his lack of family contact over the years, Jack Anderson tried to shake the lonely feeling that was newly recurrent and finished his pie.

****

Heading back into the Castwell city limits and to the hotel where he had been living, Nate Brewer drove along the highway on his way back from the Thanksgiving shift of his new job. As he passed the "Morriston Exit 1 Mile Ahead" sign, he felt his foot ease off the gas pedal. Cars passed him with honking horns as his speed was on a constant decline. With the exit less than fifty yards from where his car was on the highway, he had nearly come to a complete stop. All it took for him to slam his foot back on the accelerator and straighten his wheel was flirting with the thought of encountering his father again. The idea he had once sworn off completely had become the reason for his momentary standstill.

The seeds were sprouting.

Christmas Eve night.

With their Christmas tree aglow, Colin and his mother, Carolyn, sat in the downstairs sitting room. They were enjoying the exchange of the few gifts they had gotten for one another. Each taking turns, it was Colin's time to unwrap the next gift when he suddenly paused.

Setting the gift aside, he said to his mother, "You know, I'm glad you chose to close down the Inn tonight. I think we deserve to enjoy the big tree on Christmas Eve, you know?"

"Well, there actually just weren't any reservations; but I'd rather see it that way than as the dry spell it actually is."

"Right." said Colin, as he was thinking of the business struggles his mother was experiencing. Carolyn spoke up, "Go ahead, open your gift."

Without knowing that something else would be opened before his gift, Colin reached over to do as his mother had said. Just as he began to make the first tear in the wrapping paper, another pause came about … one he had not expected. Hearing the doorbell, he wondered if his mother had something to do with it.

Not being a fan of surprises, Colin ambivalently asked Carolyn, "Is this part of the gift?" but he knew by the look on her face that she had not expected the doorbell to ring any more than he had.

Walking toward the door, he turned and said to his mother, "You never know, it could be some last minute business."

"Well if it is, tell them we don't usually do walk-ins, but we'll be nice for the holidays and let them slide … with an extra charge of course." Carolyn said, unashamed of her desperation.

When Colin opened the door, however, the idea of a potential makeshift profit left his headspace completely. Instead, the prospect of a more substantial gain was unveiled. In addition to Charlie, there was Tony's family of five standing on the front porch. This was the sight of six fully grown seeds that had blossomed into something beautiful. They were joined together to create a bouquet in need of two more, Carolyn and Colin, to be complete. That desire had led to a quick and unplanned venture to the Webster Inn for another Christmas Eve family celebration. From the moment the seeds sprouted and broke through the ground, their growth had no limits.

That very desire had also brought the "Seed Planter" himself, Jack Anderson, back to his nephew's front door with a covered dish in hand. Joining his extended family for dinner was not the final destination of his journey, it was the first of many. The man Jack Anderson had become had subconsciously given him a new destination and he had taken the necessary steps to get there.

And as for Nate Brewer, he had maintained his speed along the highway on his way back from his Christmas Eve work shift. Without the slightest bit of thought, he took the Morriston exit. Upon seeing the street sign, he completely relinquished control of his actions and ceded to the seed growing within him. He knew exactly where he belonged as he continued on until he reached the final turn before making a full circle back to the highway and on to the Webster Inn.

Once again they were all gathered in the place where they had made so many memories in earlier years. They all enjoyed seeing the twelve ornaments they had not welcomed a few weeks earlier as they glittered in the lights from the huge Christmas tree in the corner of the room. Candlelight provided a special aura and cast just enough light to reflect on the family trunk with the three keys in their proper keyholes ... old to young. It was displayed as a centerpiece on a side table, and beside it sat the vase, where the search had begun, filled with fresh poinsettia flowers. It was the perfect setting ... and the perfect feeling ... when they all began to sing again ... *"On the first day of Christmas, my true love gave to me ..."*

Family together again.

Made in the USA
Middletown, DE
11 March 2022

62440036R00093